# DEANS BIG BOOK OF

# DEANS BIG BOOK OF

# Fairy Stories

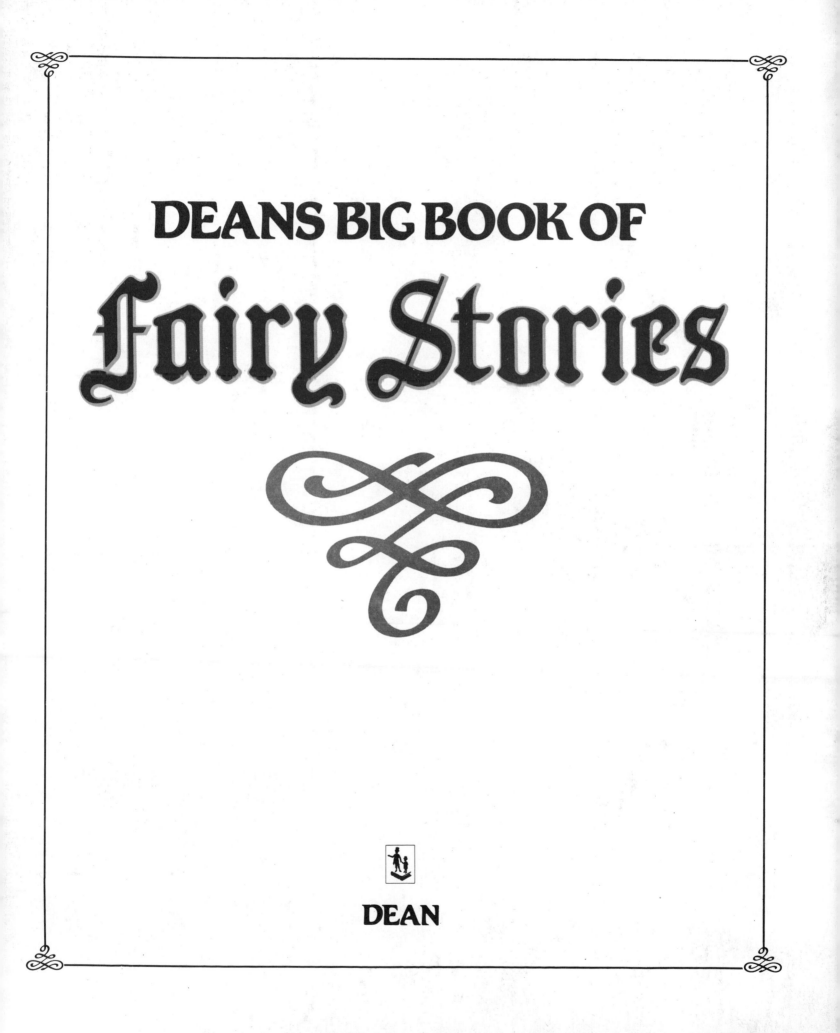

**DEAN**

First published 1985 by
Deans International Publishing
52—54 Southwark Street, London SEl lUA
A Division of The Hamlyn Publishing Group Limited
London · New York · Sydney · Toronto

Frontispiece and illustrations for *Sleeping Beauty* and *The Treasure
Casket* Copyright © Martspress Limited 1985
Remainder of illustrations Copyright © Falcon Books Inc., 1982
Text translation Copyright © Martspress Limited 1985

ISBN 0 603 00380 **X**

Printed in Czechoslovakia
52 092

#  Contents

# The Emperor's New Clothes

Once there was an Emperor who was very interested in clothes. He was always buying new outfits and he would spend hours chatting to tailors and weavers of cloth about which colours suited him best and which cloth was better for coats and which for trousers.

This Emperor's court was a happy, jolly place because he was always arranging theatre performances and throwing parties, so that he would have an excuse for wearing yet more new clothes.

Then one day two swindlers came to the court. They were dishonest men determined to get something for nothing. They told the Emperor they knew how to weave beautiful, lightweight material which became invisible to anyone who was a fool or was unfit to hold his job.

'Clothes made from that material would be

wonderfully useful to a man like me,' replied the Emperor. 'Weave some cloth and make me some clothes at once.'

The two swindlers were delighted. They asked for money in advance to buy special thread, but they put the money in their pockets and bought nothing. They sat in a room in the palace pretending to weave at empty looms.

After a while the Emperor sent his wise and faithful old minister to see how the work was progressing. To his surprise, the old man could see nothing on the looms. Of course he could not for there was nothing to see.

'Don't you like the lovely colours and the light texture?' asked the swindlers.

The poor, faithful old man didn't want to lose his job, so he agreed that the material was lovely and went back to the Emperor and told him that he had seen the material and that it was beautiful.

Everyone who looked at the empty looms feared to be called a fool or lose his job and so said the material was very fine and reported how beautiful it was to the Emperor.

The swindlers were given yet more money to make the material into clothes. This, too, they pocketed.

The day came for the Emperor to try on the clothes. Of course he could see nothing for there was nothing to see, but all the courtiers were standing round saying how wonderful the clothes were.

'If I say I cannot see them, people will think I am not fit for my job,' thought the Emperor, so he too said the clothes were marvellous and gave the delighted swindlers yet more money.

The Emperor had promised to walk through the streets in his fine new clothes, which everyone was longing to see. Off he went, but of course he was wearing only his underclothes.

Everyone stared, but no one dared say anything for fear of losing his job. Then one child said 'But the Emperor *has* no new clothes!' 'No! The Emperor *has* no new clothes!' everyone else agreed, suddenly finding the courage to speak up.

The Emperor glared. 'That child must be the biggest fool in the kingdom,' he said, but everyone knew who really was!

# The Musicians of Bremen

Once there was a donkey, who, after many years of faithful service, was cast aside by his owner. 'You are of no further use to me,' said his master. 'You are old and worn out, no good for a day's work. Off with you.'

Quite shocked by such ingratitude, the donkey decided to go right away and try his luck in the town of Bremen. He had heard that the mayor there was looking for musicians for the town band.

As he made his way along the road, the donkey fell in with a dog, a cat and a cock. All three of them considered that their master did not value their services highly enough and they wished to better their lot.

But the animals were too hungry and tired to miss such a chance of food and shelter. It was time to be bold. First, the donkey put his front hooves up on to the sill of the window. Then the dog climbed on to his back. The cat climbed on to the back of the dog and the cock scrambled on to the back of the cat.

In the flickering light from the window, they were already a weird enough sight, but when they started to sing, they were incredible.

The bandits could think only that the Devil himself was after them and off they ran.

Well pleased, the four friends promptly sat down at the table and ate all the platters clean. Then they settled down for a good sleep.

However the bandits were feeling chilly out amongst the trees. Just after midnight, they crept back. The bravest of them went indoors.

In the darkness the bandit mistook the glowing eyes of the cat for two embers in the fire. He went close for a better look and trod on the cat. Furious, the cat leapt up and slashed his face with its claws. Turning to flee, the man tripped over the sleeping dog, who plunged his fangs into him. Tearing free from the dog, the unfortunate bandit bumped into the donkey, who gave him a tremendous kick. Woken up by all the fuss, the cock started to crow.

By now the bandits were convinced that their house had been seized by an army of demons and they fled for ever.

Next day the animals found that the cellar of the house was filled with treasure. Thereafter they lived in plenty. They never did go to Bremen. They felt they were better off in the forest.

To their delight they found that they had a common love of music. The dog had a good bass voice. The cat was considered to be an excellent baritone and the cock was a lovely clear tenor. This being so, it seemed a good idea to go with the donkey to Bremen. But the road to Bremen was long and night caught them still journeying.

As the last light of day faded, the four animals found themselves in the middle of a thick forest. In the distance they could see a light shining feebly through the trees. They turned their footsteps towards the light and soon found themselves standing in front of a small house. The donkey peeped in at a window. What he saw made him shake with fright. Sitting round a table, laid with a very nice supper, were several fierce bandits, heavily armed.

# The
# Fish Prince
# and the
# Sultan's Wife

Once in a far, eastern country there lived a mighty sultan. Every day exquisite dishes of luxurious food were prepared in the sultan's kitchen. One day the sultan fancied eating fish and many fish of many types were caught by the royal fishermen and placed in the kitchen waiting to be prepared by the sultan's chef.

However one of the serving maids noticed that one small fish was very pretty and was still alive. It flapped about on the kitchen table and the serving maid felt sorry for it.

'The sultan will never miss one small fish,' thought the girl and she took it and kept it in her room in a bowl.

A few days later the sultan's wife saw the pretty fish in the bowl and was very taken with it. She carried the fish in its bowl to her own apartments and kept it as her pet.

Within a week the fish had grown so much that the sultan's wife had to find it a bigger home, and so she had a large aquarium put into her room.

However this was only a temporary solution to the problem. Soon the fish had grown so much that it needed an even bigger aquarium and then another and then another.

At last the sultan's wife took a decision. She ordered a large pool to be built in the palace grounds and she kept the fish there.

The fish was put into the pool with great ceremony and it appeared to like the pool for it went on growing and growing.

In the end it became a huge creature and a very ugly one. What was more it seemed to be an unhappy creature. When it had finished growing, instead of swimming friskily about, it moped quietly in a corner of the pool and didn't seem at all well.

The sultan's wife was very fond of the fish. She herself went to feed it twice a day.

'What's the matter with you?' she asked the fish one morning. 'Why are you so sad?'

She was only a little surprised when the fish answered her, for strange things happened in those far-off days.

The fish lifted its nose out of the water and said: 'I'm bored in this pool by myself. There's nothing to do. I should like a companion. I should like to get married. But I don't want to marry another fish. I want to marry a young woman.'

The sultan's wife was amazed.

It had never crossed her mind that a fish would want to get married. However, when she thought about it, it didn't seem so strange. If only the fish had asked to marry a trout instead of a young woman!

Still, she would do what she could to help, although the sultan's wife did not really think she would have much success.

The sultan's wife sent heralds to every part of the land announcing rich rewards for any young woman who would come to live at the palace and marry a fish. Hardly surprisingly, no one came forward.

However, in a foreign country, far to the north, there lived a horrid old woman, who came to hear of the strange offer.

This woman had a daughter of her own, an ugly spiteful girl. She also had a step-daughter, who had been born to the first marriage of her husband who was now dead. This girl, called Karin, was not at all like her half-sister. Karin was pretty and charming and good-natured.

However, Karin was not happy because she was not wanted by her step-mother nor her step-sister. She was always made to feel in the way.

On the day that the messengers from the sultan came to her house, this horrid mother was very pleased.

She saw a chance of getting rid of her step-daughter and of making some money.

'You have a marvellous opportunity to better yourself, Karin,' said the old woman. 'Go to the river and wash all your clothes nice

and clean and then pack for a long journey. You are going to live in luxury in the palace of the sultan of the next realm and I shall get a reward for letting you go. And remember to do as you are told, when you get to the palace. You must marry some pet fish belonging to the sultan's wife. Not what everyone would choose, perhaps, but you are only an orphan and must take what chances you get.'

Karin knew it was no use arguing with her step-mother and went to the river to wash her clothes, but she could not help crying.

A frog hopped out on to a stone and asked what was wrong.

When Karin told him, he laughed.

'My dear girl,' he said, 'there is no need to be upset at all. That fish is really a handsome prince under a spell cast by a wicked fairy. I will tell you exactly what you must do to make everything turn out for the best.'

He gave Karin three little pebbles.

'When you are at the palace and married and sitting alone by the pool where the fish lives, it will rise to the surface,' he said. 'When it does, toss one of these pebbles in its mouth. Then it will not be able to harm you. But be sure of one thing. Never fall asleep by the pool, or the fish will surely eat you.'

Karin cheered up after that and, clutching the three pebbles, she took her clean washing back to her step-mother's house.

Hardly sorry at leaving such an unkind home, Karin journeyed to the sultan's palace where she was given beautiful clothes, glittering jewels and a lovely house to live in – near the fish's pool.

Then the sultan's wife said: 'You must sit by the pool alone. The fish will want to come up and meet the girl who is going to be his wife.'

Karin sat terrified by the dark water. Suddenly the ugly fish stuck its head above the surface. At once Karin threw a stone between its sharp teeth. The fish sank, but in a few minutes it was back again. Karin threw the second stone between its teeth and again the fish sank away.

Now Karin had only one stone left. What should she do when this was gone?

The fish rose to the surface yet again. Karin tossed the last stone into its mouth and shivered with fear. This time the fish did not sink. There was a sound as loud as thunder and in front of Karin stood a young, handsome prince.

The spell was broken!

With the help of the sultan's wife, the young couple were married and went back to the prince's own land where they lived happily ever after. Karin's step-mother and step-sister were *furious*.

# The Seven Samurai

A great number of years ago in Japan, on the steep side of a high mountain, where black clouds swirled forever round the summit, there yawned an immense cavern. This cavern was the hideout of a band of vicious bandits.

Every night they descended to the valleys like a pack of wolves, ransacking and robbing the villages and killing anyone foolish enough to try to oppose them.

Many brave expeditions soldiered up the mountain to try to wipe out these wicked robbers. None ever returned.

The Emperor of this country had other troubles. He could not send his army after a mere band of robbers. However, he felt sorry for the poor folk living in terror. So he spoke to the noble Raiko, the most valiant samurai in the whole of Japan.

Samurai were trained from childhood to be cunning, brave, fearless, expert fighters, on their own or with other samurai.

'You may have companions and all the weapons and machines of war which you

17

think fit,' said the emperor, 'but rid my country of this brood of robbers.'

Raiko bowed respectfully before his emperor.

'Oh powerful and mighty one,' he said, 'I have no need of many companions nor of grand machines of war. The bandits would see such things coming from afar off. They know their mountain better than anyone else. Before we came near them, they would be hidden in secret caves and gulleys. But a trick —a trick could defeat them and make them helpless before me.'

This pleased the emperor and he told Raiko to defeat the bandits as he wished.

So Raiko chose six other samurai from amongst his friends. They covered their glittering armour and their costly clothes with the worn robes of holy pilgrims and started to climb the mountain.

The mountainside was wild. There were no roads. Sharp stones bruised the feet of the seven samurai as they toiled ever upwards. And the seven brave men were not walking unseen.

The watchful eyes of the bandit sentries followed every step they took. However seven pilgrims seemed no menace to the tough gang of bandits, and pilgrims were certainly not worth the effort of robbing. The samurai walked on unmolested.

At last, as night fell, the samurai came to the iron door which guarded the entrance to the great cavern. Raiko knocked on the door.

'We are poor lost pilgrims,' he said to the bandit who came to the door. 'Please give us shelter for the night.'

The band of villains were in a good mood. A side of beef was roasting over the fire and the bandits were laughing and joking.

One who seemed to be their leader beckoned to the samurai to enter. He told them that if they would sit in a corner and keep their mouths shut, they could stay the night.

The samurai crept humbly into a corner and ate the scraps of food the bandits threw to them.

When the meal was over, Raiko stood up, a flask of wine in his hands.

'We are poor pilgrims,' he said, 'but we should like to give you something in return for this shelter. Please drink this wine. Drink the whole flaskful. It is for you.'

Even though he was trying to be a humble pilgrim, Raiko could not help keeping some of the air of an important man. The robber chief jeered at him.

'Just look at this fellow offering me cheap wine with mighty airs and graces,' he laughed. But all the same he took the wine and sniffed at it. It was good wine and he could not resist drinking it, as Raiko had planned.

'Don't keep it all for yourself. Give us some,' roared the other bandits. And so the flask of wine went from hand to hand till all the robbers had drunk some and the flask was empty.

The cavern rang with their songs and laughter and the red light of the fire danced over their faces. But suddenly one after the other they gasped and clutched at their burning throats. The wine had been poisoned. They reached for their weapons, but too late. They fell and perished, every one.

The seven samurai threw off their pilgrims' robes and stood revealed in their warrior garb and gave their cry of triumph. The bandits who had terrorised the valleys were no more. Now the villagers could sleep in peace.

The descent from the mountain was long and hard, but at last Raiko and his friends were able to stand before their emperor, the Mikado as he was called, and tell him of their success.

The Mikado rejoiced greatly in the news and to show his pleasure heaped honours and titles on to the seven samurai.

# The Tinder Box

Many years ago a soldier was returning from the wars. His route led him through a forest and there he met an ugly old witch.

Being a tough soldier, he wasn't afraid of a little old lady, witch or not, so when she spoke to him, he stopped to see what she wanted.

'You're a strapping looking fellow,' she said, 'would you like to do a job and earn some easy money?'

'Everyone would like to do that,' replied the soldier. 'What do you want me to do?'

The witch pointed to a hollow tree.

'Climb down through that hollow stump and way, way down, you will find yourself in a place where you can find plenty of money. You can tie a rope round your waist so that I can pull you up again. Will you do it?'

'I suppose so,' agreed the soldier, 'it doesn't sound so difficult, but exactly how shall I get the money?'

'Well,' smiled the witch, very pleased, 'when you get to the bottom of the hole you will find yourself in a wide passage. It will be quite light because the passage is lit by a hundred blazing lamps. You will see three doors which you will be able to open because the keys will be there.'

'Go into the first room and you will see a box in the middle of the floor. A dog with eyes as big as saucers will be sitting on top of it, but don't mind that. I will give you my blue checked apron. Spread that on the floor, lift the dog on to it and he will not harm you. Then you can take as much copper money from the box as you wish.'

'However if you would prefer silver money, go into the next room. There you will find a dog with eyes as big as millstones sitting on another box. Do not mind him. Put him on my apron and take as much silver money as you wish.'

'If you prefer gold money, go into the third room. There you will find a dog with eyes as big as round towers. He is a mighty dog, but do not mind him. Lift him quickly on to my checked apron and then take as much gold money from the box as you can carry.'

'That sounds straightforward enough,' said the soldier, who was used to terrible dangers, having fought in the wars. 'But,' he added, 'what good does all this do you, old lady?'

'Oh well,' smiled the old lady, 'while you're down there pick up an old tinder box my grandmother left down there a year or so ago. The tinder box is all I want. You can keep all the money for yourself.'

The soldier tied the rope round his waist, handed the other end to the witch and went down the hole.

As the witch had said, he found himself in a hallway lit by blazing lights. In front of him were three doors. He unlocked the first door and went in. In the middle of the room, sitting on top of a box, was a dog with eyes as big as saucers.

'Good dog!' said the soldier, putting the dog on top of the witch's checked apron and filling his pockets with copper coins from the box. Then he put the dog back on the box, picked up the apron, went out, locked the door and went into the next room. On a box in the middle of the room was a dog with eyes as big as millstones.

He gazed at the soldier with a terrifying red glare, but the brave soldier said: 'Good boy!' and lifted him on to the witch's checked apron. The second box was full of silver coins and the soldier threw away the copper coins and replaced them with silver which was much more valuable.

Then he went into the third room. The dog in this room had enormous eyes as big as round towers and they rolled from side to side with a mad gleam. He was a fearsome sight.

'Steady boy, steady!' said the soldier and lifted this dog on to the checked apron. The gold was in the box as the witch had said. The soldier threw away the silver and filled his pockets and his boots and his knapsack with gold. Now he was a very rich man.

He went to the foot of the hole and called to the witch to pull him up.

'Have you got my tinder box?' she replied.

'Just a moment,' called the soldier and bending down he picked up a shabby little tinder box lying on the floor.

'Yes, I have the tinder box,' he shouted and the witch pulled him up.

'Give me the tinder box,' she said, holding out her hand.

'Why do you want a cheap tinder box?' asked the soldier.

'Mind your own business. Give it to me and be off with you,' snapped the witch, 'or woe betide you.'

'Oh, threaten me, would you?' growled the

soldier, now for the first time feeling afraid of the witch. Suddenly seizing her, he locked her in her cottage and went off with the gold *and* the tinder box.

From then on the soldier led a very pleasant life. He stopped in the first important town, rented some comfortable rooms, bought fine clothes, ate in the best restaurants and made lots of fine friends, who laughed loudly at all his jokes, no matter how many times he told them.

At last the day came when all the money was spent. The soldier had to sell his clothes and move to tiny rooms. None of his friends seemed to recognize him any more and he wondered if they might be going deaf, because they never heard him when he called to them.

The soldier sat alone in a small, cold room with only his pipe for comfort. He took the tinder box from his pocket and, opening it, struck a light for his pipe. To his amazement the dog with eyes as big as saucers stood before him.

'Ask what you want and I will bring it to you,' barked the dog.

The soldier asked for money and the dog brought him a bag of copper coins.

The soldier found that if he struck at the tinder box twice the dog with eyes as big as millstones appeared and brought him silver coins. If he struck three times, the dog with eyes as big as round towers appeared and brought him gold coins.

This was wonderful. The soldier understood why the witch had wanted the tinder box so much. Soon the soldier was back in his fine rooms with his grand clothes and all his friends recognized him again and heard him when he called to them.

Now the soldier had heard that the king had a beautiful daughter. One night, instead of asking the dog with eyes as big as saucers to bring him money, he asked him to bring the princess.

The dog ran to the palace, lifted the sleeping princess on to his back, ran through the streets with her, showed her to the soldier and then took her home again.

The next day the princess said to her mother, 'I had the strangest dream last night. I dreamed a dog with eyes as big as saucers came and put me on its back and carried me through the streets to the room of a soldier and then brought me home again.'

'Oh, yes,' replied the queen, 'did he really!'

That night the queen put a lady-in-waiting

to watch the princess. Again the dog came to fetch her, but this time the lady-in-waiting followed them and saw the house where the soldier lived and marked the door with a white cross.

Fortunately the dog noticed and after he had taken the princess home again, he put crosses on all the other doors in the street.

The next day when the king and queen and the lady-in-waiting and their soldiers came looking for the soldier, they still did not know which was his house. There were so many crosses on so many doors.

The queen was not to be outwitted. She made a silk purse and filled it with grain and tied it to the princess's back. Just before the princess went to bed, the queen cut a small hole in the purse.

That night the dog came to fetch the sleeping princess yet once more. This time the purse of grain left a trail all through the city. The dog did not notice and the next day the soldiers followed the track of the grain and the soldier was arrested.

Kidnapping a princess is a very serious crime and the soldier was thrown into a dark, damp dungeon. He did not even have his tinder box with him. For a while he was in despair. His luck seemed to have run out.

Then through the bars of the window of the cell, the soldier saw a poor boy. He called to him.

'If you would like to earn a penny, run to my rooms and fetch me the little tinder box you will find there,' the soldier said.

The boy did as he was told and soon the

soldier had the precious tinder box back in his hands again. Now he felt safe.

However he waited to hear what fate the king had in store for him.

At last the prison warder came to tell him.

'You are to be hanged tomorrow,' he said.

With the tinder box safely in his pocket, the soldier was not worried. The next day he allowed himself to be taken to the market place. The king and queen were there and a troop of soldiers and a crowd of citizens.

'Have you a last request?' the captain of the soldiers asked our soldier.

'Yes,' he replied, 'I should like to smoke my pipe.'

This was allowed. The soldier took out the tinder box.

He struck it once and the dog with eyes as big as saucers appeared.

Everyone gasped with amazement.

The soldier struck twice.

The dog with eyes as big as millstones appeared and everyone gasped with horror.

The soldier struck three times and the dog with eyes as big as round towers appeared.

The crowd screamed in terror.

'What do you want, oh master?' asked the dog.

'Chase everyone away and set me free,' ordered the soldier.

The dogs bared their teeth and rolled their fearsome eyes and chased everyone out of the market place. The soldier strolled back to his rooms quite free and collected his belongings.

However before he could leave town, the king came creeping in to see him.

'A man with such powers as you could be very useful,' said the king. 'If you care to stay here and help me when I need help, you could marry my daughter, the princess and live in the palace.'

As the princess was so beautiful, the soldier agreed and stayed in that kingdom and lived happily ever after — with the help of the tinder box.

# The Green Bird in the Golden Cage

Long ago, in the days when fairies and magicians and their magic spells were known to everyone, there lived a brother and sister.

*How* they lived was a mystery to them. Their home was a pretty castle set on a hillside under blue skies. Flowers and food grew in their garden. Unseen hands did all the work.

Books from the library opened and spoke to the boy and girl, teaching them their lessons. The children had no fear of these strange happenings because they had been used to them for as long as they could remember.

As they grew up the two young people would stand on the castle walls and look across the countryside. What they saw did not make them want to venture forth.

Everyone round them seemed to be at war. Bands of soldiers raided across the countryside, sometimes fighting each other, sometimes taking crops and burning the homes of the peasants.

When the children had been younger, the marauding bands had often looked at the pretty, untouched castle and turned to attack it, thinking that there would be plenty to steal in such a fine building.

The soldiers were right. The castle was well furnished. The boy and girl had beautiful clothes. A casket of lovely jewels stood on the girl's dressing table. A chest of gold lay in the accounts room. Gold and silver plate filled the chests in the dining room.

However no soldier ever stole anything from the pretty castle. As they drew near an invisible wall seemed to stop them. As they tried to ride forward the air became thick and dragged at them and their horses as if they were riding through deep heavy mud, but there was no mud, only the smiling, fertile countryside.

Soon word went round that the castle was enchanted and the bands of wandering soldiers did not even spare it a glance as they went on their warring way.

The girl, Philada, could remember no other way of life, but staying in the castle waited upon by magical servants. Her brother, Paul was older. He could remember a pretty woman who was their mother and a handsome nobleman who was their father and the ruler of the castle.

Paul could remember servants chatting about their work round the castle. He could remember the castle gates being open and laughing visitors coming to see his parents and weary travellers seeking shelter for the night.

Often Paul would look at a beautiful statue in the courtyard of the castle. It was so real it seemed that a lovely woman had stopped still as she walked and become frozen in stone.

'Mother! Mother!' Paul would murmur. 'I'm sure you are our mother. Why do you stay still and frozen? Why are we living in this circle of enchantment?'

Then, one summer, as the brother and sister watched from the walls, they noticed a difference. No bands of raiding soldiers were to be seen. A few peasants came back from their mountain hideouts and rebuilt their cottages and cultivated the land.

To their surprise one morning, Philada and Paul saw a page riding towards their castle. Nothing stopped him. He came right up to the gate and called to them.

'The wars are over,' he said, 'my master Lord Greybeard has defeated the invaders and brought peace to the countryside. He is a wise and clever man, but he cannot solve the mystery of the Green Bird. His court magicians tell him that only you who live in the enchanted castle know the answer. He has sent me to ask you to go to him and solve the mystery.'

Philada and Paul were delighted that the wars were over. They were pleased the magic wall seemed to have gone. Now they could go out and meet young folk their own age and live like normal people, but they knew nothing about a green bird. What should they do? They did not wish to anger Lord Greybeard.

Then they heard a sweet voice calling to them. Turning they saw the statue step down to the ground and its skin blush pink as life came back and melted the chilly stone. It was their mother.

'The wars are over and so is the enchantment,' she smiled. 'Many years ago, your father rode off to war with our servants. I heard he had been killed and the grief turned me to stone. You two children were left alone, but the magician of the mountains took pity on you and put a spell on the castle so that you would be safe until the wars were over.

'Then he sought out your father as he lay wounded, but still alive and turned him into a green bird in a golden cage. He promised that your father should sing safely in the cage till the wars should be over and then we should all be a happy family again.

'Anyone who tried to touch the bird before then would be turned to stone, but when one of you children runs to the cage and says: "Father" everyone will be restored to their proper form.'

Overjoyed, Philada let the page show her where the green bird sang in its golden cage on the mountainside.

'Father,' she called. At once her father stood before her and the stone statues became men again. So all had been saved from the war by the kindness of the magician of the mountain.

# The Good Deed Ill~repaid

One day a simple old peasant found himself in a wood. He had just set about collecting dead wood to take home for his fire, when he heard a cry for help. He looked up, but he couldn't see anyone, so he went back to his wood collecting.

But the cry came again. The peasant took a better look around this time and he found a snake trapped in a hole.

The peasant jumped back with fright. Snakes could be dangerous. However the little captive started to plead:

'I beg you to come to my help, kind sir. Please help me to get out of this hole.'

'Well, I could do it all right,' replied the peasant, 'but why should I? You will just come out and strike me with your poisoned fangs. You are a snake when all is said and done.'

'Oh, for goodness sake. I wouldn't do a thing like that,' said the snake.

So really against his better judgement, the peasant lifted a big stone which was half covering the hole and allowed the snake to slither out.

Immediately the snake struck at him. The peasant only just managed to jump out of the way in time.

'There you are,' gasped the peasant. 'You are a snake and I knew you would do that, but why you repay a good deed with a bad one, I can't think.'

'For a very good reason,' replied the snake. 'It is the way of the world. A good deed is *always* repaid with a bad one.'

The peasant didn't agree with him.

'Everyone isn't like that,' he said. 'Why, if someone does me a good turn, I remember it and try to repay it with another good turn as soon as possible.'

The snake just scoffed.

'I'll make a wager with you,' he said. 'Find a single being who agrees with you and I promise never to try to strike you with my fangs again.'

So the peasant and the snake set out together. Walking along the road they met a worn-out old horse hardly able to drag one foot along behind the other. His hairy old tail flicked half-heartedly at the flies which tormented his skinny flanks.

The peasant asked him: 'In your opinion, my good horse, in the ordinary run of things, how is a good deed repaid?'

The horse didn't hesitate.

'With a bad one,' he neighed.

'Why ever do you say a thing like that?' asked the dismayed peasant.

'Because,' said the horse, settling into his stride to tell a good story, 'when I was young

and strong my master looked after me well.'

The horse went on: 'My master lodged me in a fine stable and gave me as many oats as I could eat. But now I am old and feeble, he has completely cast me aside. No nice stable and no more oats for me!'

'There you are,' said the snake, quite satisfied, 'now it's all right for me to strike you with my fangs, isn't it?'

'Well, just hold on a moment,' hurriedly replied the peasant. 'I think we ought to ask someone else as well.'

They went back on their way and soon saw a sheep in a field. The peasant decided to consult him: 'In your opinion, my good sheep,' he asked, 'and in the ordinary way of things, how is a good deed repaid?'

'By a bad deed,' said the sheep, hardly bothering to look up.

'But why do you say such things?'

The sheep scowled: 'Because from the moment I started giving wool to my master, he decided to leave it on my back during the summer, so that I fainted with the heat and to clip it off in the winter, so that my bones freeze.'

The snake reared up.

'That settles it,' he said. 'I can strike you now with my fangs.'

'Don't be hasty,' gasped the peasant. 'There must be other points of view.'

So on they went and fortunately the peasant caught sight of a fox before the snake did and slipping aside had a word with him.

'In a moment I will come and talk to you with a snake,' he explained, 'all you have to do is to say that a good deed is rewarded with another good deed and later I will give you a lamb, a sucking pig and a fat goose.'

'That sounds like a good offer,' replied the fox and so it was arranged and the peasant went back to walk with the snake.

Soon they met the fox. 'In your opinion, my good fox,' said the peasant, 'and in the ordinary way of things, how is a good deed repaid?'

'By a good deed,' smiled the fox, thinking of the lamb and the sucking pig and the fat goose. Then the three of them fell to chatting and the fox heard how the snake had been trapped in the hole and he refused to believe it and they all went back to the hole and the snake went back down the hole to show the fox how he had been trapped and at a nudge from the fox, the peasant rolled the stone over the hole and he never had to fear the snake again. The fox had done him a really good turn.

But that evening when the fox went to the peasant's farm, he found the lamb locked safe in the sheep pen, the sucking pig shut in the pig sty and the fat goose in the chicken house and the peasant chased him away with a gun and two fierce dogs.

'Well, you live and learn,' puffed the fox. 'That snake was right after all!'

# The Magic Candle

Once upon a time, in a mighty kingdom, there lived a soldier called Mark. Mark was a brave man and had risked his life a thousand times on the field of battle in defence of his king.

One day, when the king was passing in procession with all his grand courtiers, Mark stepped forward. He bowed low.

'Sire,' he said, 'I have fought for your majesty for many years, but now, I haven't even enough to live on. Could I dare hope that you would give me a modest pension?'

The king was furious at being bothered.

'How dare you be so impertinent,' he shouted.

'Get out of the way or I will have you beaten and put into prison.'

The soldier went back to his poor room, stripped his uniform from his back, took up his trusty sword and set out to find his fortune on the open road.

After tramping for many weary hours, the soldier came to a dark wood and in the wood he saw a hovel. It was the home of a witch.

The witch said she would give Mark shelter for the night if he would descend a deep well and fetch for her a candle which burned with a blue light. Mark agreed and he got into a large basket which the witch lowered down the well by means of a rope. Mark found the candle and the witch started to pull him up again. However the witch was planning to trick Mark.

'Pass up the candle to me,' she weedled, 'and then I will pull you the rest of the way up.'

But Mark was as cunning as she was.

'How do I know that you will pull me up?' he asked. 'After I have given you the candle you will not need me any more.'

The witch flew into a rage and let go of the rope. 'Think it over at the bottom of the well,' she shouted.

Fortunately Mark was not hurt and to calm his mind he started to smoke his pipe which he lit from the candle. No sooner had he lit the pipe than a little black goblin appeared before him.

'Your word is my command,' the goblin said.

Mark was astonished, but quickly said: 'Get me out of this place.'

The goblin not only whisked Mark and the candle from the well, but supplied him with treasure and a fine house in which to live.

'If you need anything, just light your pipe from the candle and I shall appear,' he said.

Mark enjoyed a fine life for a while, but then he remembered the shabby way in which the king had treated him. He lit his pipe at the blue flame of the magic candle and said to the goblin: 'Fetch me the king's daughter.'

When the unfortunate girl appeared in his house, Mark made her work as a servant for

a day, then sent her back to the palace.'

The king was furious and when his daughter told him she had left one of her silk slippers under a cupboard in the strange house, he sent his soldiers to search until they found it.

Mark was captured and condemned to death, but he asked for a last request, which was of course to smoke his pipe, which he lit from the candle.

When the goblin appeared, Mark ordered him to take up a cudgel and beat the guards and even the king himself. This soon made the king see things in a different light. He pardoned Mark, gave him his daughter in marriage and became a good and patient man.

And the goblin?

Well, he continued to be a good friend to the soldier and his wife and brought them all they ever needed to make their lives happy.

# The Princess and the Big Test

Once upon a time, in Bohemia, there lived a powerful prince who had an only daughter. The girl was called Diomira and many young men of the very best families came to ask for her hand in marriage.

However Diomira was rather fussy. This young man was too tall and thin. That one was too short and fat. This one had a red nose. That one had big ears.

There was just no pleasing her.

However her father, the prince, was growing old and tired.

'You must marry,' he said to Diomira. 'I need a son-in-law to help me rule my lands and a grandson to inherit my title.'

Diomira sighed. She knew she would have to marry one day, but she would like to marry someone handsome and clever and charming. So far she had seen no one she liked at all. They were all plain and boring.

She thought of a plan to put off her marriage until she found someone she really cared for.

'Father,' she smiled, 'I will marry a noble lord if he can pass this test. He must sit with me in a closed room for three hours and not let me escape. If he can do that, I will marry him.'

Her father was well pleased. This seemed a simple test. How could a girl escape from a closed room? He sent for several suitable young men to come and try their luck.

However, the test was not as simple as it appeared. The nurse of Diomira was a sorceress. In the flickering of an eye she could change the girl into a flower or a bird or any creature large or small.

The young men arrived and sat in a closed room in the palace with Diomira and her nurse, however closely they watched the young lady, she always managed to disappear.

Then Lord Matos came to the palace. He did not come alone. With him he brought three very useful companions. First there was Longshanks. He could reach as far as the eye could see. Then there was Firebrand. He

once the nurse muttered another magic word. Diomira became a little fish and leaped into a goldfish bowl.

Again it happened so quickly that no one could see but Hawkeye. Again he told Lord Matos what had occurred. This time the young man turned to Firebrand. He whispered in his ear and pointed towards the glass goldfish bowl.

Firebrand smiled and breathed towards the cool glass. In a few seconds his hot breath had cracked and shattered the bowl. Only Longshanks' long arm was able to stretch out and catch the fish before it fell to the ground.

Longshanks put the fish back on the chair and at once it became Diomira.

It was almost the end of the three hours. It seemed that Lord Matos had passed the test. Then the nurse's lips moved and Diomira became a bird flying away through the window. Hawkeye spoke to Lord Matos. He

could scorch things with his breath. Finally there was Hawkeye, who could see even the very swiftest of movements.

Handsome young Lord Matos and his three companions sat in a closed room in the palace. Opposite to them sat Diomira and her nurse. For half an hour all was stillness.

Then in the blink of an eye the nurse whispered a magic word and Diomira became an apple and rolled away under a cupboard. It all happened so quickly that no one saw it.

No one but Hawkeye. He whispered in the ear of Lord Matos. Young Lord Matos told Longshanks to stretch his long arm to take the apple from beneath the cupboard and put it back on Diomira's chair.

At once Diomira resumed her proper form.

Another hour passed by. Lord Matos became drowsy. He yawned and blinked. At

sprang to his feet, drew his bow and, with unerring aim, brought the bird down with an arrow through its wings.

At once the bird became Diomira, whole and unharmed.

The three hours were over. Lord Matos had passed the test. Diomira had to marry him.

The Prince of Bohemia, Diomira's father was delighted. Lord Matos was from a very fine and wealthy family. He would be an extremely suitable son-in-law.

Truth to tell, Diomira herself was not sorry Lord Matos had passed her test. He was charming and handsome and obviously clever to have brought such useful companions with him.

Diomira chose a beautiful wedding dress and the marriage took place with much feasting and parties lasting for days.

The poor people were given food and wine and it seemed that everyone in the land was happy.

However Lord Matos did mention that he thought perhaps it was time for Diomira's nurse to retire to a nice cottage in the country.

No doubt he felt a sorceress would be an uncomfortable companion, if he wanted to live happily ever after with Diomira.

# Valentine and the Sword of Light

Valentine was not born to be a hero. He was strong and calm and good, but that is a long way from being a dashing knight in shining armour.

He loved his own country, yet he enjoyed travelling. He had to be free, not caught down in dull routine.

His joy was a fine little boat in which he explored the uncharted seas, fearing neither storm nor pirates.

He needed no one and nothing, but his own skills and his own strength.

One year, as usual, Valentine went away on a long trip, living by fishing and hunting.

Exploring round the coastline, he came to the entrance to a great river. He worked his way quite a few miles upstream, when suddenly, to his great surprise, he heard someone calling to him by name.

He looked up and saw a tall, proud, old man standing under a tree. The old man had the calm air of someone who had stood there for many a long year watching time roll by.

Intrigued that the man should know his name, Valentine beached the boat and jumped ashore. 'You don't know me, Valentine,' smiled the old man, 'but I am your father's brother. I knew that you would pass this way eventually and I have been waiting for you for many a weary hour. Thank goodness you have come at the time when your country needs you.'

Then from beneath his cloak, the old man drew out a sword which burned like the sun and glittered like ice.

'This sword belonged to your father,' said the old man. 'I have been guarding it since his death. Now I must give it to you. It will make you invincible. You must use it to save your country which is in terrible danger.'

Valentine was amazed. Such a thing had never happened to him before. He did not know his father had a brother. He was even more astonished when the old man disappeared like a wisp of smoke caught in the wind.

Valentine took the sword and continued his journey upstream. He could think of nothing else to do. But then unseen hands seemed to pull his boat to the side of the river. It was moored in a little sidestream. Valentine was pulled ashore into a wood. He walked on hesitantly, taking the sword with him hidden in a cloth.

Suddenly he saw a magical and terrifying horse. Its coat was brilliant green and its eyes flamed fire-bright in the first shadows of evening.

'Mount on my back, oh master,' the horse said to Valentine, 'and I will take you to where you are desperately needed to save your country.'

Poor Valentine! Little had he thought such an adventure would befall him when he turned his small boat upstream to explore the river.

He mounted the snorting, restless horse and wondered what would become of him.

At once the horse set off on a crazy, wild gallop. It raced across plains and pounded through villages which Valentine had never seen before.

On and on for swaying, crashing mile after mile it went, until at last in the far distance, Valentine saw the towers of a huge city. As he approached, he saw that the towers were burning.

As he drew closer still, Valentine saw that an enormous army was camped all around the city. He saw hundreds of tents and many horses and guns. Then he drew near enough to see the men themselves. They were enough to strike terror into anyone's heart.

They were mighty and strong and they wore fine, glittering armour with narrow slits where their eyes should be. They looked like men accustomed to fighting and winning.

The horse circled the town and paused on a hill so that Valentine could see the whole army spread out before him.

'You must save the city and save your country,' neighed the horse. 'You can do it with the help of the sword of light.'

Valentine took the sword from its cover of cloth and then with one mighty sweep, he drew it and whirled it round his head.

His heart filled with courage. He knew no fear. Those mighty knights now looked like so many blades of grass to be swept before him.

The horse neighed and pawed impatiently. Valentine shook the reins. The horse charged into the centre of the large enemy army.

What a terrible sight it was for the enemy soldiers. Suddenly from nowhere a green horse with blazing eyes, neighing and snorting raced in amongst them. Sitting on the horse's back was a young man free from fear, as brave as a lion, waving a sword which shone like the sun and glittered like ice.

'Who is he?' 'Where has he come from?' they asked each other.

They didn't know whether Valentine was friend or foe. They didn't know whether to fight him or to obey him.

'Has he come out of the city?' they asked. 'We saw no gate open,' others replied.

By the time they realized that Valentine was an enemy, they were in such confusion that panic spread through their ranks.

The fantastic horse charging amongst them and the fearless rider on its back, with his flashing powerful sword set them all to flight.

The poor folk inside the besieged city watched with amazement. When they saw that the tide of battle had been turned, they came surging out through the city gates and drove the enemy army far, far away, so that it never dared to return.

Through all the turmoil and battle, not a blow, not a scratch fell upon Valentine. He had rushed into the thickest of the throngs of his enemies, but nothing had harmed him.

As had been promised by the old man standing at the side of the river, the magic sword of light had made Valentine invincible.

He had defeated the enemies of his country and he had been unharmed himself.

The leaders of the city ran to greet Valentine.

'You are our saviour,' they said, 'without you the whole city would have been destroyed.'

They invited Valentine into the city and lodged him in the most beautiful palace and gave him honours and riches. They wanted him to take command of the army and stay with them for the rest of his life.

But a change had come over Valentine. He

was no longer the quiet, calm young man who had been happy pottering about exploring and living by hunting and fishing.

'I have held the sword of light in my hand,' said Valentine. 'I have ridden the green steed with the blazing eyes. I cannot stay here where the battle is won. I must seek other battles.'

Valentine rode away from the city.

'I must use these wonderful gifts to defend the weak and the needy,' he said, 'only send for me if you are in great danger.'

Valentine had become a hero.

41

# Rose White and Rose Red

The world has not always been as it is today with towns and villages and roads and open fields. Not so very long ago, thick forest and woodlands spread for mile after mile after mile.

The few rough, dangerous roads led *round* the densest woods. Only a few narrow tracks went into the deep forest itself and these were mostly used by hunters or woodcutters . . . or . . . or . . . or *what?*

The forests were dark and mysterious. All the trees looked alike to a stranger. It was easy to get lost amongst the thickly growing leaves and branches. And what wild animal or fairy creature might be lying there in wait?

But then, no place is frightening if you have grown up there and it is your home. Many years ago there was a woodcutter's cottage in a little clearing a mile or so within a forest. The woodcutter had died, but his widow still

lived there quite happily with her two daughters Rose White and Rose Red.

The girls had grown up in the forest. They knew exactly what was safe to do and what was not. They knew the ways of the animals and how to avoid making them angry. They knew all the pathways and animal tracks for miles around their cottage. And so these good and clever little girls were able to walk out into the forest and so they had this adventure.

The whole affair started one very cold winter, when an enormous bear came knocking at the cottage door. Normally it is wise to keep away from bears, which are extremely big and strong.

However this bear spoke in a human voice and called out and asked if he could shelter by the cottage fire.

The snow was blowing a blizzard and for sure the bear would perish if it stayed outside, so the mother of Rose White and Rose Red said the bear might come in and keep warm. They opened the door and the bear entered.

For all its huge size, the bear was gentle and well-behaved. Rose White and Rose Red brushed the snow from its fur and the bear slept by the fire and departed in the morning.

Every night during that bitter winter the bear came to the cottage for shelter. He and the two girls became quite friendly.

Then spring came. The snow stopped falling. The frosts were not so hard. The bear said:

'I must go back to my haunts in the deepest woodlands. I shall not come to visit you again till next winter.'

And he left. However as he went a strange thing happened. He caught his fur on the door latch and tore it and underneath the fur it seemed to Rose White that she saw the gleam of gold.

However the bear was gone and could answer no questions and the girls went on living their lives and enjoying the warmer weather.

Then one day, when they were out picking berries, they saw a dwarf with his beard caught in a tree trunk.

The dwarf was shouting and tugging and beating on the tree and was really in a state of great distress. The two girls hurried closer.

'Can we do anything to help?' they asked kindly.

'Of course you can,' snapped the dwarf,

'and the first thing you can do is to stop gaping at me like idiots.'

This seemed a very ungrateful way to talk, but the kindhearted girls still stayed to help the bad-tempered little fellow.

'I put a wedge in the tree trunk to try to split it open for firewood,' said the dwarf, 'but the wedge sprang out and my beard was trapped. Can you put the wedge back again?'

Rose White and Rose Red knew they were not strong enough to drive wedges into trees, but Rose Red suddenly remembered that she had a pair of scissors in her pocket. She took them out and snipped off the end of the dwarf's beard.

'There! You are free!' she said, thinking the dwarf would be pleased.

'You horrid girl. Fancy cutting my beautiful beard!' he snarled. 'Be off with you before I really lose my temper.'

Actually he was not really cross. He wanted to drive the girls away so that they would not see the treasure he had found in the tree trunk. He did not want to share any of the gold pieces with anyone.

The girls hurried away and thought no more of the cross little dwarf until some weeks later. Then they were gathering wild herbs near a river when they heard shouting and splashing and saw the same dwarf. He had been fishing and had hooked a very large fish, but in the struggle the dwarf's beard had become tangled in the fishing line. Now it seemed that the fish might pull the dwarf into the river.

Taking her scissors from her pocket, Rose Red stepped forward and snipped the dwarf's beard from the fishing line.

Again instead of being grateful, the dwarf was angry. 'Couldn't you have thought of a better way of saving me than cutting my beard?' he shouted. 'Go away, you silly creatures.'

This time the dwarf had a bag of pearls with him and didn't want to share any with the girls even though they had undoubtedly saved his life.

One would have thought that by now the girls would not do a good turn for anyone, but a few days later they saw a creature struggling in the talons of an eagle. At once they caught at the unfortunate struggling victim and after a terrific tussle, pulled it free.

It was the dwarf.

This time the dwarf was right outside the entrance to his treasure cave and he was afraid the girls might glimpse all the riches inside.

'You have torn my clothes to tatters, pulling at me like that,' said the ungrateful little wretch. He began to beat the girls with a stick hoping to drive them away.

But he chose just the wrong moment. The bear was passing and heard the cries of Rose White and Rose Red. He ran up and felled the dwarf with one blow. Then there was a flash of light and the bear's skin fell away to reveal a king dressed in gold. How happy he was.

'I never knew which dwarf had put the spell on me,' he said, 'but as I am free it must have been this one. Had it not been for you two girls calling to me, goodness knows when I should have managed to break the spell this dwarf cast on me so he could steal my riches.'

So the king shared the riches from the dwarf's cave with the girls and they all lived happily ever after.

# The Alpine Flower

The Queen of the Snows is the most beautiful fairy spirit in all the world. Many years ago, she lived in the high mountains called the Alps.

Where the mountains were tallest and the snow deepest, there in a huge grotto cut from the ice, the Queen of the Snows had her palace.

Everything was white. Blinding, glittering light dazzled everywhere. The great hall was walled with mirrors of polished ice. Every reflection was multiplied a hundred times, so that the hall seemed to be thronged with people if only one were standing there.

Every sound bounced to and fro between the hard frozen pillars. One little word brought a thousand voices echoing back.

Mountaineers and the shepherds who lived on the lower slopes of the mountains risked their lives to climb up to see the beauties of the dazzling palace.

Those who were lucky saw the palace and retraced their dangerous paths to safety. However those who were unlucky saw the Queen of the Snows.

This creature was so beautiful that everyone who saw her fell in love with her. Their love was all in vain. It had been written in the great Book of Fate that the Queen of the Snows should never marry mortal man.

The Queen of the Snows had a heart of ice. She did not care whether these scrambling climbers loved her or not. However it amused her to talk to them. She liked to sing and these silly mortals were an audience for her lovely voice as she sang as prettily as the wind sighing in the pine trees.

When the Queen of the Snows was tired of the men who came to gaze at her, she called to the goblins of the rocks. They crawled forth from their frozen crevices and hustled the unfortunate mortals away down the treacherous, frozen slopes, not caring whether they reached the valleys in safety or not.

One day a good and handsome young hunter was out tracking mountain goats, when he heard the lovely voice of the Queen of the Snows blowing down across the snowy rock-face.

He could not resist climbing up to see who could possibly be singing in such a terrible place.

He entered the ice-bound palace and saw the beautiful Snow Queen. He fell in love with her at once, but being a modest young man did not tell her so. He thought such a beautiful woman could never be interested in a humble hunter like himself.

This was such a change from the protestations of undying love the Queen of the Snows was used to hearing that she became interested in the young hunter. In fact she fell in love with his modest charm and he stayed in the glittering palace, walking and talking with the lovely queen and staring deep into her eyes.

The goblins of the rocks saw what was happening. They were furious. The Queen of the Snows must not marry mortal man. They crawled out from amongst the rocks and seized the young hunter and threw him back down the mountain to live with mortals, where he belonged.

If the young man ever tried to climb back up the mountains, the goblins of the rocks stopped him.

They hurled rocks. They sent avalanches of snow roaring down the valleys.

They never let the young man come near the Queen of the Snows again.

At last the love of this valiant young man wore thin.

'I am wasting my life seeking something I can never have,' he sighed.

He turned back to the valley and married a farmer's daughter.

The Queen of the Snows searched in vain for the young man she had loved so much.

'He is gone,' laughed the goblins. 'He didn't like it up here in the cold. You are better off without him. It is no use relying on mortals.'

Even the frozen heart of the Queen of the Snows was broken. For the first time ever, warm tears slid from her eyes. They ran down on to the rocks and slithered along the lips of the caverns. There they turned into silver stars, which nowadays grow as flowers. We call them edelweiss and they are said to be the most beautiful flowers in the mountains.

# The Well of Dreams

Long, long ago, in a castle in Scotland there lived a young boy called James. James would often play with a little girl called Julie, the daughter of his nurse.

One day in autumn, a terrible storm raged for days and the two children could not go out into the park to play, as they usually did. To keep them amused, the nurse decided to tell them a story.

'This is a true story,' she said, as the three of them settled in front of the fire.

'Near this very castle, at the top of a hill,' went on the nurse, 'there is the Well of Dreams. If you stare long and hard into its furthest depths you will see things more wonderful than anything on this earth.'

She went on to describe all the visions which the local farmers said they had seen in the well's dark waters.

James was so excited he didn't sleep a wink all night. He got up at dawn, slipped out of the house, climbed the little hill, peered into the depths of the Well of Dreams. And from that moment no one saw him again.

Years passed by. Julie grew into a young woman but she never forgot her little childhood friend. One day she wandered to the top of a nearby hill and found herself staring at an old well. She remembered the stories her mother used to tell.

'Can this be the Well of Dreams?' she thought and leaned over the edge and peered into the well's grey depths.

At first she saw nothing unusual, but after a while the water of the well became more and more transparent, as if a bright light were coming to the surface.

The young girl saw beautiful gardens, a huge castle with a hundred towers and banners blowing in the breeze. A grand procession of lords and ladies came from the castle. At the head of the procession was a young man. Julie recognized him at once.

'James!' she called.

The castle and the gardens shivered. The water of the well boiled in turmoil. The young man struggled to the surface of the well.

After ten years James had returned.

When James stood in front of his parents once more, they wept for joy and asked where he had been for so many long years.

'I stared into the Well of Dreams,' said James, 'and saw the most beautiful nymph. She smiled at me, took my hand and led me down into the water. We went to a mighty castle full of grand folk and feasting and parties. But then I drank from a forbidden flask. Everything changed. The nymph became a toothless hag, the grand folk became ugly gnomes and dwarfs. I was a prisoner amongst these hideous people till a faithful friend would lean over the well and call my name.'

How grateful James was to Julie and how happy to be back amongst friends. And he never, never again peered into the depths of the Well of Dreams!

# The Peasant and the Three Thieves

Once upon a time there was a real old simpleton. He lived in a small village in the countryside near the eastern city of Baghdad. He was so simple, he believed everything anyone said to him. Even the smallest village children were able to take him in with their tricks.

One day this poor old country bumpkin decided he would go to the market in Baghdad to sell his goat. In those days poor people had to walk everywhere, so it was several days' journey to Baghdad.

What a performance the old man made of getting ready. It took him a week to make up his mind how much food and what clean clothes and how much water he would need for the journey, but at last he was ready.

He packed his supplies on the back of his donkey and he tied the goat to the donkey and round the neck of the goat he tied a bell.

The old man thought this was very clever. 'As I walk along I can listen to the bell

ringing,' he thought. 'While the bell is ringing I know no one has stolen the goat.'

In those days there weren't so many people as there are now. The countryside between villages was wild and lonely and dangerous.

The old simpleton started on his journey and, of course, in a lonely place three thieves were waiting. They watched the old man go by.

'I will steal that goat,' said one.

'Then I will steal the donkey,' said another.

The third thief was disgruntled.

'That just leaves his miserable clothes for me to steal,' he grumbled. 'Still, I suppose that is better than nothing.'

So the first thief waited until the old man paused for breath as he went up a steep slope. Then the thief crept out from behind a bush, cut the rope which tied the goat to the donkey, took the bell from the goat's neck, tied it to the donkey's tail and crept swiftly away.

The old country bumpkin went happily on his way, listening to the bell ringing and thinking that the goat was still safely trotting behind.

After a little while, however, he did look back and was amazed to see that the goat was not there, even though the bell was ringing. He hurried back and found the bell tied to the donkey's tail and then even he realized that he had been well and truly tricked.

How he wailed and shouted!

Just then a second man approached him. Of course, this was the second thief. 'What is the matter with you, my good man?' he asked. 'Why are you shouting and screaming so?'

'My goat! My goat! First it was here. Now it is gone. Someone has stolen it,' groaned the old man.

'Really!' said the thief. 'Then you are certainly in luck that you met me. Only a few moments ago, I saw a man dragging a goat along, as if the goat didn't want to go with him. It was over there, behind that clump of trees on the other side of this field. Why if you ran, I believe you could catch up with them in no time.'

'Oh thank you. Thank you,' beamed the old man. 'I will run after them at once. But will you do me a big favour and look after my donkey for me while I am gone?'

'A pleasure,' smiled the second thief and held the reins of the donkey while the village simpleton ran away across the field.

Needless to say, he did not find his goat behind the clump of trees and when he got back to the road, out of breath and exhausted, his new friend was gone and the donkey with him.

The old man wept and wailed and tore his hair, but there was no help for it. His goat was gone. His donkey was gone and with the donkey all his food and water and supplies. There was nothing for it but to make his way home as best he could.

The road was long and hard and dusty, and the sun was high and hot in the sky. The unfortunate old man was glad when he came at last to a well. Sitting by the well was a man moaning and tearing his hair, just as our friend had done.

'I'm ruined. I'm lost,' he wept, sobbing and making a terrible fuss. The old man went up to him, and asked:

'What is the matter with you?'

'I am in the most terrible trouble in all the world,' wept the man by the well. Our old man could scarcely believe that. He could think of nothing worse than being robbed of first his goat and then his donkey. However he went on listening.

'I leaned over the well to pull up some water,' said his new friend, 'and I dropped a purse full of precious stones belonging to the Caliph of Baghdad. If I go to the Caliph and tell him I have lost the stones, he will fling me into prison.'

The old man had to agree.

'Yes, that certainly is bad trouble,' he said, 'but why don't you go down the well and fetch the purse of precious stones? You should be able to find it easily enough.'

'Oh, I can't swim. I am afraid to go down the well,' said the third thief — because of course that is who it was. 'However,' he went on, 'there are ten pieces of gold in the purse, as well as the precious stones and I will give the gold to anyone who would fetch the purse up for me.'

The old man was thrilled. Ten pieces of gold would buy another goat, another donkey, more supplies and plenty left over.

'In that case I will go down the well and look for the purse,' he smiled. 'But I don't want to get my clothes wet. Will you look after them for me while I go down the well?'

'A pleasure,' said the third thief and took the clothes, as the old man climbed over the parapet of the well and lowered himself down towards the water.

The water was icy cold and felt even worse to the old man who had just come out of the hot sun. Nevertheless, in he plunged and felt around in the mud, trying to find the purse. He didn't want to disappoint his new friend waiting anxiously at the top of the well.

However, he *found* no purse because there *was* no purse and when at last he climbed out of the well, there was no man waiting and there were no dry clothes waiting either.

It took him some time to realize that he had been robbed yet again. Very upset, he went home shouting and bewailing his ill luck to everyone who would listen. But things did not turn out too badly. His neighbours thought it was such a funny story they kept inviting him to dinner to tell it all to them. And for months the old man had free meals all round the village in return for recounting how he had been fooled three times over.

# The Great Empress

Many years ago, the islands of Japan were in turmoil. A great and wicked noble had risen in revolt against the Empress Jowka.

The noble, called Ti-Lu, was a samurai, a warrior trained in all the arts of war. He was a clever general and when his battle skills failed him, he resorted to magic, of which he was a master.

Many traitors flocked to his banner encouraged by his success. His armies conquered vast areas of Japan, looting and burning and making slaves of all the people.

At last Ti-Lu and his followers stood before the capital itself and the Empress Jowka called her generals to a council of war.

'High and mighty empress,' said the bravest amongst them, 'nothing can stop this traitor. His sorcery can overcome the bravest of our soldiers.'

This was a terrible thing to say, but the rest of the generals agreed. They knew no way of stopping Ti-Lu.

Empress Jowka dismissed them and sat alone overcome with grief. The stories from the towns and villages occupied by Ti-Lu were horrifying. He behaved like a wild animal, yet she, the empress to whom everyone looked for guidance, could think of nothing to do to help.

That night the empress went to her bed-chamber, but she could not sleep. Suddenly a soldier appeared before her.

He was upright and strong, but he was old and his long beard was completely white. In the dimness of the room his magnificent armour sparkled with light and the sword which he held in his hand glittered with an eerie brightness.

'I am the God of Fire, Jowka,' he said, 'your grief has touched me and I will help you defeat your enemies. Tomorrow I shall set myself at the head of your armies and my powers will overcome all the magic tricks of Ti-Lu.'

Overjoyed, the Empress Jowka threw herself at the feet of the God of Fire and thanked him for all he intended to do for herself and her people. She had scarcely spoken when the earth shook, a red fire filled the room and the God of Fire was gone.

The next day Jowka sent for her most able general. She ordered him to equip an army and get it into the field in the greatest haste.

In a flurry of surprise, infantry and cavaliers put on their armour, readied their arms, sharpened their swords, until, at last, everything was prepared. The general led his men to parade in front of the empress.

Jowka caught her breath, when, riding at the head of her men, she saw an old samurai with a long white beard. His air was proud and confident. She knew him at once. It was the old man who had come to her room in the

night. It was the God of Fire keeping his promise and riding at the head of her soldiers.

At last Empress Jowka began to believe that the rebel Ti-Lu would be defeated.

Meanwhile Ti-Lu was in his tent preparing for battle. He had not the slightest fear of the army which was coming against him. His troops were brave and experienced. They believed in the lucky star of Ti-Lu, which had already brought so much success. So many men had flocked to his banners that his followers were more numerous than a swarm of locusts.

Ti-Lu stood on a hill and watched the columns of his enemies marching towards him. For this final throw Jowka had called on her every last resource. Truly Ti-Lu had never seen such an army come forth against him, but he had no fear. He had complete faith in his own men — upheld by their valour and his magic powers.

The two armies ranged themselves face to face and prepared for battle. Shouted orders rang out over the lines of men as the bravest and most desperate samurai in Japan waited to hurl themselves at each other and scream out their terrible battle cries.

Everyone knew that this was the last battle. The fighting rolled to and fro with both sides determined to win, but so bravely did Empress Jowka's troops fight, that by dusk the outcome of the battle was certain. Ti-Lu would be defeated.

But Ti-Lu was still unafraid. Now was the moment to use his magic powers. The army of the Empress Jowka was spread out across the plain. If a wave of water engulfed the plain, nothing could save them.

Ti-Lu pointed his hand and a mighty spout of water burst up from the earth. It poured across the plain in a mighty surge. It seemed that Jowka's great army was going to be destroyed in its moment of victory.

But then, as if cut by a sword, the swirling waters parted. Ti-Lu stared in disbelief, as a wide path appeared in the midst of the waves and marching up it came the old man who had appeared to the Empress Jowka.

After the old man strode the victorious general and his escort, garbed in splendid armour, upright and proud. No water dare so much as lap at their feet. It shrank back and swirled away as if driven by an irresistible force.

The tables were turned. This time there was no safety for the armies of Ti-Lu. They were surrounded and made prisoner. All the sorcery of the rebel samurai was helpless against the power of the God of Fire. Soon, alone and desperate, Ti-Lu turned and fled.

He drove his horse until it dropped and then he found himself on foot on the slopes of a high mountain. He started to climb upwards from rock to rock, and all the while he was pursued by the enemy general and his bodyguard. The hot sun shone down on him without pity and for all his tricks and magic ruses, his enemies stayed close behind him.

At last he came to the summit of Mount Shu. He was about to be captured. Soon he would be the prisoner of Empress Jowka, chained up, shamed and jeered at.

Black despair seized the soul of Ti-Lu. He howled like a madman and rent his clothes. Then with one last great act of will, he crashed his head against a rock and gave up his life. The mighty, wicked rebel had been finally defeated.

But that was not the end of Ti-Lu's magic. He had struck the peak of the mountain with such force that it splintered into fragments. Huge blocks of stone which a hundred men could not move were broken into a thousand tiny pieces. In an instant the top of the mountain disappeared and in its place yawned a mighty crater from which poured fire and burning stones and huge clouds of black smoke.

Down in her beautiful palace the Empress Jowka learned in the same moment of the victory of her army and of the new horror which was befalling her country. Immediately she called together the council of elders.

The wisest of the old men spoke: 'Grand Empress,' he said, 'we should not be surprised at these terrible happenings. They often occur on the death of someone practised in the arts of black magic. It is as if the forces of evil are taking vengeance for the loss of one of their faithful servants.'

'That may be,' replied the empress, 'but what can I do to remedy it?'

Her councillors were not able to give her any very practical advice.

'Be brave and patient yourself,' they said, 'and your subjects will be brave and patient too.'

Jowka followed this advice because she could think of nothing else to do, but fire and flames continued to pour from the mountain top. It seemed that the whole country would be engulfed in a winding sheet of molten lava. On and on poured the river of fire.

At length the burning river reached one of the pillars which held up the sky itself. It surged round the base, melting it with searing heat and the pillar shifted and tumbled to the ground with a shock which echoed round the world.

Part of the sky cracked and fell to the earth. Dark shadows loomed over all mankind. The paths of the sun and the moon were torn across and they could no longer drive on their accustomed routes to bring light to the earth by day and by night. All the time darkness reigned, bringing cold and death.

Everyone was very frightened at this constant darkness. People stayed indoors, not daring to go out, even to look for food.

Empress Jowka asked advice from astrologers and from learned men and they suggested many things, but not a single one of their ideas was of any use at all. The only good idea came from Jowka herself. She ordered huge fires to be lit. They were so large that whole trees were cast on them at a time. And although even these great fires were like little candles in the great darkness, yet they brought some comfort to the frightened people.

Then Jowka sat and thought hard and long. At last she made up her mind. She ordered heralds to go to all the villages and towns in Japan. They ordered all her subjects old and young to bring to the empress every stone of the following colour: blue, orange, red, white and black.

Men and women, children and old folk found and carried the stones to the gardens of the empress.

When the Empress Jowka considered that enough stones had been collected, she ordered huge cauldrons of water to be boiled over the great fires, which were already burning. Then she had the coloured stones cast into the boiling water together with the finest powder of porcelain which could be found in the whole of Japan.

The fires were kept at roaring heat by teams of volunteers anxious to help their empress.

The contents of the cauldrons formed into a sort of paste and every now and then Empress Jowka had some brought to her. She examined it carefully and at last it was soft enough and brilliant enough to please her.

Jowka lifted her eyes to the dark sky. A small cloud was floating close above her head.

'Little cloud,' said the empress, 'it has fallen to your lot to take me up to the spot where the sky is broken.'

The cloud agreed and carried Empress Jowka and the huge cauldrons of paste high into the air, right up to the place where the

sky was torn and broken. Using the glittering, glowing paste, Empress Jowka mended the damage in the sky. Then, still riding the cloud, she went down to the sea and captured a huge turtle.

The turtle formed a strong base for the fallen pillar and soon it was standing again, supporting the mended sky and the empress's work was done.

Or so she thought. To her despair, the empress realized that, although she had repaired the sky, the sun and the moon still had not reappeared.

Again the Empress Jowka consulted her wise men and again their advice was useless, until she spoke to an old man who lived alone on a tiny island, eating nothing but fish and fruit.

'I think,' said the old man, 'that the sun and the moon are at ease in their palaces, not bothering to look to see whether the sky has been mended or not. Someone must go to tell them.'

An ambassador was sent at once. 'Good heavens! Is the sky really mended?' gasped the sun and the moon. They had thought the sky so badly damaged it could never be repaired. How they admired the clever work of the wonderful Empress Jowka.

So the sun and the moon harnessed their horses and again rode their chariots across the sky, bringing light to the world by day and by night. The earth came back to life and the people prospered.

From every corner of the land, people came to thank Empress Jowka for her clever deeds. Modest Jowka said she had merely done her duty.

# The
# Witches' Wood

In many ways the King of Navarre was a fortunate man. His kingdom was prosperous. His subjects were content. No enemies were attacking the borders of his land. Yet the king was sad. The whole court was plunged in gloom.

The king's daughter, Princess Maria, was ill. Every day she became paler and weaker until it became clear to everyone that she was fading away. The king sent for all the wisest doctors in the realm. None could cure the princess.

All the people of Navarre felt sorry for the king, but there was nothing they could do to help. They had to carry on with the business of making a living.

One young man called Carlos worked as a goatherd. Every day he took the goats to graze on the mountainside and every evening he brought them back and locked them up in a shed where they would be save from wolves and wild mountain cats.

However, one evening when Carlos was shutting the goats away for the night, he found that one was missing.

Carlos was very annoyed. Now he had to go back through the falling darkness to search the hillside to find the missing animal. In the night it was easy to trip over a boulder or a fallen branch and to hurt oneself, let alone

find a straying animal. However the job had to be done and Carlos walked back towards the wood which surrounded the foot of the mountain.

Carlos was walking as carefully as he could amongst the trees, when he saw a strange glowing light coming from a little way off on

his left. He was surprised. This certainly was not moonlight and he had seen no signs of gypsies camping. He crept across to investigate, after all, his goat could be attracted by the light too.

It was as well that Carlos had been cautious. The bright light came from a flaming throne on which was sitting a wizard. In front of the wizard were standing a group of witches. Their appearance was ugly and cruel and wild. Carlos shivered.

The wizard on the throne took out a red book and checked through the pages.

'I hope you have all been carrying out the wicked mischief I set for you to do?' he said, glancing round the group of horrible witches.

'Oh yes, indeed we have,' they cackled, 'yes, and with a will, too. Doing evil is our delight.'

Carlos' blood ran chill. He crouched down hardly daring to breathe in case these frightening creatures discovered him.

'Yes,' spoke up one witch, 'I set fire to a field of ripe corn. What a lovely blaze it made.'

'I made the mayor ill after eating his wife's pie, so he blamed her for it,' screeched another.

'And I am still making Princess Maria ill,' chuckled another hag, 'but the best part of that is that the cure for her illness is at the palace itself. There is a turtle under the main water pipe of the palace. If the princess sipped turtle soup for three days running, she would be cured.'

The wizard laughed with approval.

'No one will ever tell her of that cure,' he said and he snapped the book shut.

'You are all doing magnificent wickedness,' he smiled. 'Be off with you and meet me again in a week.'

The witches and the wizard hurried away. The flaming throne disappeared and Carlos was left alone in the darkness. Only the sound of the goat bleating brought him back to his senses. He took the goat home and tossed restlessly in his bed for the rest of the night.

The next morning Carlos told his younger brother to tend the goats and Carlos himself set out for the royal palace.

It is not easy for a goatherd to get into a palace to speak to a king. However Carlos' manner was so sincere and his face so honest that first the guard took him to the sergeant, then the sergeant took him to the officer. Then the officer took him to the minister for the army and the minister for the army took him to see the master of the royal household and finally Carlos was ushered in to speak to the king himself.

'Give the princess turtle soup!' gasped the king. 'How ridiculous! As if a simple thing like that could cure her!'

'It is soup from a special turtle,' explained Carlos. 'The soup must be made from the turtle under the main water pipe of the castle. Perhaps that turtle has been eating a special plant which will help cure the princess. I don't know. I only know for sure that drinking the turtle soup will cure her.'

The princess was so ill that the king was desperate. He ordered the turtle to be found and made into soup. As Carlos had instructed, the princess was made to take sips of the soup for three days.

At the end of the three days, the princess was cured. She was up and about with her cheeks rosy and her eyes sparkling.

The whole court rejoiced.

The king sent for Carlos and thanked him and Carlos told him the whole story of how he had seen the meeting of witches in the wood at the foot of the mountain.

At once the king sent for holy men to say prayers through the land and particularly in the wood and, as far as anyone could tell, the witches never bothered anyone again.

However, ever afterwards the wood was known as Witches' Wood and no one went there unless he had to.

As for Carlos, he was invited to live at court and made a fine career in the army and eventually married the princess whose life he had saved.

# The Man with the Horse's Head

Once upon a time a rich old man lived in a magnificent home in Brittany. But this man who seemed so fortunate was bowed down with grief at the fate of his only son, Irwin. Irwin was healthy and clever, but he had been born with the head of a horse!

However, although this was tragic there seemed to be no help for it and Irwin was brought up as normally as possible. When he reached the age of twenty, his father said he should marry and the father went to visit a farmer who had three pretty daughters.

The eldest girl agreed to marry the monstrous Irwin because he was the son of a rich man.

'When we are married, I shall kill him and then I shall be a rich widow,' she thought.

The day of the wedding arrived, but the next day, it was not Irwin who was found dead, but the girl.

The man with the horse's head persuaded his father that the girl had deserved her fate.

'I only did to her what she tried to do to me,' he said.

The second daughter of the farmer heard that her sister had died of illness.

'Good,' she thought, 'now it is my chance to become rich.'

So the second daughter married Irwin and alas the same fate befell her as had befallen her sister.

Now it was the turn of the youngest girl to marry Irin. She had no plans to kill the young man and in fact when she knew him she came to like him. In the course of time a normal healthy baby was born to the happy couple.

The man with the head of a horse was overjoyed. He kissed his wife and said:

'Tomorrow, when our child has been baptised, I shall be freed from the spell which made a monster of me. But the enchantment will not cease until the last sound of the church bells has died away. You must not say a word to anyone about the spell being broken until the service of baptism is finished completely.'

Naturally the young woman was very happy at this news. She promised to say nothing until the church bells had stopped ringing. However promises are easier made than kept.

The next day the girl's mother came to see her. The baby was christened and the church bells rang. The girl was so happy. The bells would stop ringing at any moment, surely it was safe to tell her mother the good news about Irwin.

So the girl told her mother that Irwin had been under a spell, but that now, the spell would be broken and he would have the head of a normal man.

Alas, the girl finished speaking and then the bells stopped ringing. She had told all her news before the bells had ceased.

Irwin came bursting into the room where the girl sat with her mother. He was in a terrible state of distress and disarray.

'What have you done, Marian?' he groaned — Marian was the girl's name — 'Now I must go away to a far place and never be free of this horse's head.'

'Oh, forgive me,' begged Marian, clutching at her husband. He pushed her away and the violent movement made three drops of her blood fall from her nose and land on his white shirt.

A terrible voice called: 'Take the wife of the man with the horse's head to the Mountain of Crystal.'

At once a huge bird of prey seized Marian in its talons and carried her so fast she could scarely catch her breath, across the width of a sapphire sea to the foot of the Mountain of Crystal.

Poor Marian looked in despair at the steep slippery slopes and the one house at the peak of the mountain. Then a fox took pity on her.

'Hold on to my tail,' it barked, 'and I will help you up to that house. A very unhappy man lives there. A man with a horse's head.'

Marian took heart. This must be the house to which her husband had been exiled.

With the help of the kindly fox, she reached the house and saw three washerwomen washing a shirt. On it were three drops of blood.

'Nothing we do will get this blood out,' they complained. 'Our master will be furious with us.'

'Let me try,' said Marian. With one gentle rub she made the shirt clean. The washerwomen were delighted and helped Marian to get a job as a servant in the house. That night Marian hid herself beneath her husband's bed.

When he came in, she stepped out and said:

'I am the one who cleaned the spots of blood from your shirt, but don't you recognize me?'

Overcome with joy, Irwin took Marian in his arms and at oncc his horse's head disappeared and he became a handsome young man. The spell was broken.

The next day Marian and Irwin left the sad, cold house and went back to Brittany, where they lived with their child, happy ever after.

# The Parrot Prince

Long, long ago, in the days of old, a Shah of Persia died. This Shah had one son, a young man called Mansur and this young man came to the throne.

As befits a young man, Mansur was adventurous and bold and full of ideas to do great things.

This did not please the old Grand Vizier, who had been adviser to Mansur's father.

'Going on wild adventures will do the country no good,' he sighed. 'These things cost money, but if the people have to pay high taxes they will become discontented and rebellious.'

He sat and pondered what he should do.

Meanwhile Mansur himself wished to make plans for how he should rule his new realm. He went to the temple of the God of Wisdom where a huge flame roared forever upwards, carrying prayers up to the spirits in the sky.

'I know I am young and rash,' whispered Mansur, 'but give me guidance to do what is right.'

Of course, he hoped to be told to do something adventurous. Sitting in the palace going over tax accounts and checking that the roads were kept in good repair might be very necessary, but it was boring.

Then one day when Mansur went to the temple, he heard a voice speaking to him from the roaring flames.

'You are a grown man,' said the voice, 'you must do what your own wisdom tells you. Yet one wish will be granted to you to help you with your many tasks.'

Mansur asked that he be given the power to change into any other creature, man or beast

and then, when he wished, return safely to his own body.

His wish was granted.

Mansur went back to the palace and spoke to the old Vizier.

'The voice from the flames told me I should do as I think best,' he smiled, 'and also I have the power to turn into any sort of creature I wish.'

The old Vizier was horrified.

'Now Mansur has been told to do as he wishes, he is sure to go dashing off on some mad scheme and perhaps be injured,' he thought.

However, the Grand Vizier was a clever man. It was clear to him that if Mansur could fall in love with a suitable princess and get married, he would be much more content to stay at home. And once he had children, he would want to look after them and would not be so eager to rush off risking his own life.

But how could the Vizier make finding a wife seem like a great adventure?

Then the Vizier heard of the perfect princess. She was good and beautiful and the right age. Her father was king of a neighbouring kingdom and he was wealthy, but best of all, marrying the princess would be very difficult indeed.

The king, her father, was very jealous of the princess. He liked hearing her sing in her enchanting voice and he liked the jolly parties she arranged and the way she ran the palace so that nothing ever went wrong and his meals were always tasty and on time.

The king did not want the princess to get married. He wanted her to stay at home always.

The Grand Vizier spoke to Mansur.

'King Tibur in the kingdom over the mountains has a daughter just suitable for you to marry,' he said, 'but he has said that no one may marry her. He has surrounded his palace with seven dense walls of sharply pointed spears and every night the princess and her maidens sleep in a place where no one can ever find them.'

At the talk of the seven fences of sharp spears, Mansur's eyes had lit up. Overcoming such a barrier would be a daring feat for a young man.

The Vizier went on. 'In the garden of King Tibur's palace is a mighty pomegranate tree. It carries three fruits. Every evening the tree bows its branches down to the grass and the three pomegranates open wide.

'In each fruit is a feather bed large enough for a human person to sleep inside. The princess gets into the middle bed and her two maidens-in-waiting get into the beds on either side. Then the fruits close and the tree lifts its enormous branches till they wave up high in the sky and brush the stars. No one can reach the princess till morning.'

Mansur was following the Vizier's every word, so the old man went on.

'King Tibur has said he will put to death anyone who tries to steal the princess and marry her.'

This made up Mansur's mind. Winning and marrying this princess must be a great adventure and folk would talk of it for years.

Mansur ordered a parrot to be brought to him. Summoning up all his powers of will and concentrating his thoughts, suddenly he became the parrot and his own body lay on a couch in his room waiting for his return.

The parrot flew out through the palace window. It flew over the high mountain separating Mansur's realm from that of King Tibur. It shivered as it felt the cold blowing up from the glittering snow on the high peaks, but on it flew.

Mansur in his parrot form saw the rich Kingdom of King Tibur far beneath him. He came to the palace surrounded by the sharp cruel fences of spears. He flew above them, not daring to think of what would happen if he fell down on them from exhaustion.

By now it was evening. The mighty pomegranate tree was bent down to the lawn. The princess and her maidens were stepping into their feather beds.

The three pomegranates closed tight and the branches started to rise. Before they could spring up high, Mansur darted forward. With his parrot's beak he pecked through the stalk of the pomegranate and carried the fruit away with him. It was heavy and with his tired wings, the prince could only just clear the razor-sharp spears. His claws dragged wearily in the snow as he crossed the high mountains, but he reached home safely with his burden.

In a moment he was back in his own body again and the princess was stepping from the pomegranate, truth to tell glad to have escaped from her dull life shut up in the palace.

Soon she and Mansur were married, while the Vizier was making everything well with King Tibur. And Mansur was content to stay at home and rule his realm.

# The Red Dragon

Many, many years ago, a simply enormous red dragon lived on the earth. The red dragon was discontented.

He called all the other animals together and spoke to them.

'This world is a dangerous place,' he said. 'Men hunt us and persecute us. Above the clouds is a beautiful country where nothing can harm us. If you care to climb on my back I will take you there.'

At once there was a terrific scramble to get on to the red dragon's back. The lion soon stood back. He was king of the forest and he thought it was beneath his dignity to push and shove amongst his subjects.

The tiger did not bother with the dragon's plan at all. The tiger loved excitement. She thought the battle with man was a glorious, dangerous game.

The dragon soon realized that he could never carry all the creatures swarming over his back.

'Some of you, please get down,' he begged, 'you are far too heavy. I shall never get off the ground, let alone fly above the clouds.'

The elephant glared at the hippopotamus. 'You should get off, you great big bag of munched up grass,' he said.

The hippopotamus was furious.

'You're a fine one to talk,' he said. 'You're as light as a feather, I suppose.'

The giraffe spoke up.

'I think the rhinoceros should get off,' she said. 'He is the heaviest.'

'But I got on first,' replied the rhinoceros indignantly. 'It's not fair if I have to get off. I'm not moving for anyone.'

The crocodile was determined not to get off either. He looked round.

'Let the hyena get off,' he said. 'Nobody likes him anyway.'

The hyena soon snapped back.

'Oh — and I suppose *you* are everybody's favourite, then!'

The butterfly was the only reasonable one.

'I'll go on the next trip,' she said, fluttering from the dragon's back.

'Good. That's settled then,' said the elephant, watching the tiny butterfly go. 'Someone's got off, dragon, so get started at once.'

'Yes. That's right,' said the crocodile. 'Stop whining, dragon. You invited us to get on after all. Up in the air with you.'

The dragon, struggled and puffed and panted and finally lumbered into the air. It got as far as the tops of the trees. Then it realized it was far too heavily laden. It would fall to the ground itself if it did not get rid of its burden.

With a shake of its shoulders, it sent all the animals falling to the ground. Fortunately they all fell into long grass and did not really hurt themselves. However that fall made some big changes, which have lasted to this day.

The crocodile landed on all fours and pushed its legs into little short stumps. The elephant swallowed lots of air and blew up its body and forced its nose out long. The muzzle of the hippopotamus squelched in some mud and became covered with lumps and its eyes

screwed up small.

The giraffe caught its head in the fork of a branch and stretched its neck. The snake slithered along and lost its legs and feet completely. And the wisdom tooth of the rhinoceros bounced out of its mouth on to its nose.

And that is the story of how the animals came to be as they are today.

What happened to the big red dragon is something about which no one is very clear.

Perhaps he did fly away and never came back. Perhaps he did come back and is living in some deep and distant forest. Perhaps he will come back for a visit any day now. It might be worth keeping an eye on the sky in case he is flying around anywhere.

# The Legend of the Grey Lake

Edward was the bravest and most gallant of all the knights of ancient Spain. Nothing could deter him from saving damsels in distress and rescuing orphans from wicked stepfathers.

On and on he went, over mountains, through valleys, slaying monsters and putting terror into the hearts of wicked men.

He was big and tough and strong and valiant, as everyone knew because he never stopped telling them so.

'Just point me in the direction of an adventure,' he would say, 'and I will show you how to wield a sword and ride a horse and put the enemy to flight.'

Edward was very happy leading this wandering adventurous life.

'All this outdoor exercise keeps a hero fit,' he used to say. 'And I like seeing new faces and new places all the time. A knight can't be a stick-in-the-mud, can he?'

So Edward journeyed onwards with his faithful squire Alfonso and really people were very grateful to him for all his good deeds. And then they were just as grateful when he moved on. He was so boisterous and restless

and forever wanting to stir up excitement, looking for dragons round every corner and wicked witches under every bed.

However the time came when Edward was really out of luck. He crossed a range of mountains with Alfonso and came down into a land where there was no trouble at all.

Everyone lived in peace and happiness. There were no monsters fiercer than a cat, and the duke of the region was virtuous and kind.

Edward, and Alfonso too, became very bored. They rode through the length and breadth of the land and could find no adventure at all.

At last, after a long day's ride, they came to an inn where they stopped for a meal and a bed for the night.

They had seen nothing but happy faces all day long and now, here at the inn, everyone looked plump and well-fed and content. It obviously wasn't even worth asking if there were any fire-breathing dragons in the neighbourhood.

Edward sat sunk in gloom.

'I shall be glad when I have had enough of this dukedom,' he sighed. 'I hope we are near the border and can ride out soon, or I shall fade away with boredom.'

Little did he know that the most perilous adventure of his life was almost upon him!

Edward was actually a great and rich nobleman and he was dressed accordingly.

He and Alfonso had not been sitting eating for long, when a pale, willowy young man dressed in white robes and who looked as if he had never done a day's work in his life came to speak to them.

'Do you mind if I share your table?' he asked. 'I can see that you are people of quality and I should love to talk to you instead of having to make do with the clods and country bumpkins who live round here.'

Edward nodded and the young man sat down.

'I am a poet,' he said, 'but no one round here is clever enough to appreciate me.'

Actually the poor young man was out of luck because although he was educated and a nobleman, Edward was no more interested in poetry than the local farmers.

'But I'm glad you spoke to us,' he said to the young poet. 'You don't happen to know if there are any adventures in these parts, do you? Are there any mysteries which only a brave man could try to unravel?'

At first the young man shook his head, but then he said: 'Well, there is always the mystery of the Grey Lake, but,' he looked doubtful, 'you are a fighter and I don't know that the Grey Lake is your sort of mystery.'

Edward was so bored that he felt any mystery was better than none.

'Tell me about the Grey Lake,' he begged.

'Well,' said the young man, 'a few miles to the west is a lake with cloudy slate-grey waters. They never clear. No one can ever peer into their depths. However on the night of the full moon a beautiful young woman rises from the depths of the lake and calls for someone to walk across to her.'

The young man laughed: 'Of course no one ever does. How would they walk on the

water? And would they ever come back again? However, sir, if you wish to do something daring, which has never been done before, answer the call of the lady of the Grey Lake.'

Edward was delighted. It didn't sound as if there was going to be much fighting, it was true, but this certainly was an adventure.

The next day, in spite of Alfonso's objections, Edward rode to the Grey Lake and, dismounting from his horse, kept watch at its side until the night of the full moon.

Sure enough, when the moon was high in the sky, the most beautiful girl he had ever seen rose to the surface of the lake and beckoned to him.

'Come to me. Come to me,' she called and her voice was the sweetest in the whole world.

Edward was filled with wonder and started to walk across the water and the water took his weight. He walked as if he were on land.

The beauty of the girl and the white moonlight and the music of a breeze singing in his ears quite turned Edward's head. He forgot about Alfonso waiting on the lakeside.

The girl smiled the sweetest smile Edward had ever seen. 'I am the Queen of the Grey Lake,' she said taking his hand.

The Queen of the Grey Lake led Edward down to the deepest depths, but he felt no cold nor lack of air. They floated together through a gateway of emeralds and a second

of rubies and a third of flashing diamonds and then they came to a palace full of beautiful people. Edward and the Queen were married, and life was laughter and leisure and parties and jolly chatting.

This was what the Queen of the Grey Lake wanted. This was why she had sought a human husband.

The other pretty young people in the magical palace had never been anywhere else. The Queen had heard all their stories before.

'Tell me about when you slew the dragon,' she said to Edward, 'and tell me about rescuing the king's daughter and tell me about defeating the bandit army of Tuscany.'

For a while Edward did enjoy telling all these stories, but then, as he always did, he became restless. Talking about exciting deeds was no use to a man of action. He needed to be off fighting again.

But when he suggested such a thing, the Queen of the Grey Lake fell into a fury.

'And what am I supposed to do while you are gone?' she snapped. 'Spring-clean the palace out, I suppose!'

'Make up your mind to this, Edward,' went on the Queen. 'If you try to escape from this palace you will drown. Your job is to stay here and keep me happy and if you don't, it will be the worse for you.'

Of course that was no way to speak to a man like Edward. He decided to escape regardless of the risk.

Whatever Edward was, he was certainly brave.

'Nothing shall keep me a prisoner, least of all a woman,' he roared. He strode from the palace. He strode through the gate of flashing diamonds, through the gate of rubies and through the gate of emeralds and found himself struggling in deep icy, grey, suffocating water.

There was a crashing and a shrieking as the palace collapsed behind him, but Edward was too concerned with trying to struggle to the surface of the water to pay much attention.

Then a large fish swam to his side.

'Hold my tail,' it said. 'I will lead you up to the air. By daring to oppose the Queen of the Grey Lake, you have destroyed her power and set us free from her tyranny and I will save you.'

So Edward reached the surface of the lake and scrambled ashore.

To Edward it seemed he had been gone for months, but to Alfonso waiting on the shore, only a few minutes had passed.

Soon Edward was dry, in warm clothes and quite his old self again. He and Alfonso rode off looking for new adventures, but definitely not in a lake this time.

# The
# Unkind Giant

Deep down in the rocks which lie beneath the surface of our earth, there are many mighty caverns. No daylight can shine down there. No fresh breezes blow, but folk do say that there is life down there. Folk do say that goblins and elves and even giants live in those huge, ancient caves.

One story says that many years ago a mighty giant called Magnus lived in a great palace carved out of the rock. Magnus ruled over a tribe of goblins who were very clever at working precious metals and finding valuable gems such as rubies and diamonds.

His underground palace was very beautiful. The hard-working goblins fashioned lights from rubies and wrought gold. They beat silver into pretty patterns to decorate the walls of Magnus' palace. They sewed elegant clothes made from fibres found in the earth and with gold and silver thread woven into them.

The giant, Magnus, had no work to do. He ruled his kingdom of goblins and told them what to do and they served him. They dared not do otherwise, he was so huge and strong. However the giant was good-tempered and fair and the goblins felt they could well have a worse master and they stayed content with Magnus.

Now it happened that thousands of years before, Magnus had been taken on a visit to the surface of the earth by one of his giant uncles.

This had been in the days before the great flood, when most of the world had been wild and natural and there had been very few people about. Magnus had enjoyed being in the sunshine and feeling the breezes blowing

from the sea. Suddenly he decided to visit the surface of the earth again.

This time Magnus had no uncle to accompany him, so he took one of the elves for a little holiday in the sunshine.

They climbed up through long narrow passageways until they came out into the light through a cave amongst some high mountains.

How amazed Magnus was when he looked around. How the surface of the earth had changed. Herds of sheep and goats grazed across the slopes of the mountains. Miles of forest had been cleared and farm buildings and neat fields covered the countryside. Every now and then a cluster of houses and a church showed where a village had formed. In the distance Magnus could see a large grouping of many small and great houses which was a town.

'Who has made all these changes?' gasped Magnus.

The elf pointed at the human beings who could be seen moving and working everywhere across the landscape.

'Those creatures, smaller than your highness, but larger than I am, must have done all this,' he said.

The giant was very interested to see what these creatures who had done so much work could be like.

'I will pretend to be one of them and live amongst them for a while,' he said to the goblin, 'you go back to my underground kingdom and say I shall return after a few weeks.'

As always the goblin did as he was told and the giant, who had magic powers, made himself the size of a strong man and walked across to the nearest farm.

He asked for work and the farmer took him on as a farm hand.

From dawn till dusk Magnus was expected

to work in the fields. It seemed to him he only stopped for a rest now and then, but his master was always grumbling at him.

Of course the farmer lived in the comfortable farmhouse and Magnus was given a bed in a small cottage. The farmer sat at the head of the table at mealtimes. Magnus sat at the far end and was served last.

Magnus did not stop to think this was just how he treated his goblins and considered he was a good master.

'I will not put up with this,' he thought and sought work with a keeper of cattle.

Again Magnus was given a lowly room in which to sleep, while the master lived in a nice house, just as Magnus lived in a palace and his goblins lived in small rooms.

Again the best food was served to the master and plain fare was all that reached Magnus. He was disgusted.

'What a way to treat *me*!' he fumed. He left this job too and went to work for a judge in the town. However he was no better pleased here. He thought the judge was unfair to poor people and only worked in law so that he could live richly himself.

'I am very disappointed in these human beings, they are horrible,' said the giant. 'I am going back to my underground kingdom where I am a good master and not like these selfish humans.'

He resumed his giant shape and back he went. However he did not invite the goblins to live in his palace, nor eat his specially nice food.

'Those goblins do not work as hard as I did when I was a worker, so they do not deserve any better treatment,' he thought.

He did not realize that work seems hard when you are doing it yourself and less hard when you order someone else to do it. He was as unkind a master as the masters up on earth. Very few people can see their own faults.

# The Squabbling Goldfish

One summer a fair came to the town where Johnny lived. Johnny went to the fair with his father and while they were there Johnny's father won three goldfish.

The fish were from far away, warm, southern seas. Two were yellow with black stripes and one was red.

Johnny was very pleased with the fish. He took them home and put them in water in an old goldfish bowl which he found in the attic.

However, if Johnny was pleased, the fish were not. They did not like being imprisoned in a small round bowl. Two flips to the right, two flips to the left and they had been everywhere there was to go in their tiny home.

They became very bored. They kept bumping into each other. They were far from content.

The red fish spoke up first.

'This looks a very nice house,' he said, peering through the glass. 'Johnny and his mother and father are well-dressed. They sit down to a good meal each evening. This room has very nice furniture. The family can't be short of money. They could easily afford to buy us a nice big aquarium in which to live.'

'I daresay,' replied one of the yellow fish,

'but will they? They probably think we are quite happy in here. Cosy I expect they call it.'

'Well, then we must teach them otherwise,' smiled the red fish. 'You never know what you can do until you try. Just listen to me.'

The red fish explained his plan to the others.

The next day when Johnny came to sit by the bowl and watch the fish, he was astonished to see that they were squabbling.

The yellow fish nipped at the red fish's tail and chased him round and round the bowl. Then the red fish turned back and chased the yellow fish, snapping at them as he went.

Johnny became alarmed.

'Mummy! Daddy!' he called. 'The fish are squabbling.'

Daddy came to look.

'So they are,' he said thoughtfully. 'Perhaps they need a bigger home.'

That very day he went out and bought a spacious aquarium. He put plants and pebbles in the water. Then he transferred the fish. They were much happier and never squabbled again.

In fact they had never squabbled at all. They were very clever fish.

However, after a while the fish even became tired of their new aquarium.

'What we need,' said the red fish, 'is a nice fish pond.'

He looked out at the garden.

'I see the family is building a very pleasant stone terrace,' he observed. 'A wide cool fish pond, where the dappled shade of the tree falls, would be very pleasant. 'Don't you both agree?'

'We do indeed, but how can we make little Johnny understand what we want?' they asked.

'Oh, that should not be too difficult,' smiled the red fish, who was quite clever. 'We must all do some acting,' he said. 'We must behave as if we aren't getting enough fresh air. Maybe that will make Johnny think we should be outside.'

That afternoon the fish kept a sharp lookout for Johnny, who was on his way home from his Grandmother's.

'Here he comes,' bubbled the yellow fish, who had very good hearing.

In a few more moments Johnny came hurrying into the room. At once he went to the aquarium to look at his pets, the fish. He was horrified to see them floating on the top of the water gasping for air.

He called his mother in alarm.

'Try changing the water,' she suggested.

Johnny changed the water hurriedly. The water he put in was cold and the fish were not at all pleased.

'You and your clever ideas!' grumbled the yellow fish. 'All we are going to get is a bad cold.'

'We must keep trying,' persisted the red fish.

So, after shivering for a bit in the cold water, the fish went back to the surface and once more pretended to be gasping for air.

Johnny's father came in.

'I think those fish need more air,' he said.

The red fish grinned.

'I told you so,' he hissed to the other fish. 'I told you my plan would work.'

'I'm tired of bothering with them,' said Johnny's father. 'Let's throw them into the river.'

And he did.

Now in some ways this was better for the fish because they could swim where they wished. However, in other ways it was not so good. Their food was not given to them every day and sometimes they were in danger from big fish.

By doing as the clever red fish said though, they found their way back at last to the warm seas where they had been born.

Unless you are clever, it is sometimes best to be content with the life you have.

# The Princesses in the Well

Once upon a time there were three princesses who lived with their father in his grand castle.

In those days, people grew most of their own food. In the grounds of the castle were kitchen gardens for growing vegetables and soft fruit, ponds for breeding fish, hutches for rabbits, little houses for chickens and, of course, a large orchard where apples grew. There were many fine trees in the orchard, but one particular tree always produced the most luscious looking fruit.

The three princesses were very annoyed that their father always forbade them to eat any of the apples from this particular tree.

'That tree has been here since my grandmother's day,' the king would say, 'and she told me that anyone who eats an apple from that tree will vanish away and be imprisoned far underground.'

For years, while they were little, the princesses believed this story, but one autumn, when the tree was laden with crisp, shiny apples, one princess said:

'I just don't believe that story about vanishing away to an underground prison if you eat apples from this tree. Things like that don't happen any more. There may have been goblins and fairies and magic in Grandma's day, but not nowadays, I'm sure. I think father just tells us that old story so that he can have these best apples for himself when we aren't looking.'

The other two princesses agreed. They stretched out their hands and each picked an apple and ate it.

The apples were delicious, but as soon as they were eaten, there was a flash of light and all three princesses vanished. The story had been true after all.

Naturally the king was very upset. He promised that whoever could find the princesses and bring them safely home could marry one of them and live in plenty for the rest of his life.

At once three of the palace servants decided to try their luck at finding the three unfortunate girls.

They set out early one morning, searching in all the local caves, thinking that here might be a path to an underground cavern.

However they had no luck, until the youngest servant called Martin met a goblin.

'If you are looking for three imprisoned princesses,' said the goblin, 'go to the top of that mountain where you will find a deep well. At the bottom of the well are the girls, but be very careful for they are guarded by a dragon with nine heads.'

Martin gulped with dismay.

'But,' went on the goblin, 'the dragon is the least of your worries. Beware of treachery from your two companions.'

Then the goblin disappeared.

Martin hurried back to the other two servants and told them the princesses were in the well at the top of the mountain. He did not believe what the goblin had said about his two friends being treacherous.

The three servants found the well, and Martin, being the smallest, was lowered down it. Sure enough, there were the princesses and there was the dragon.

Fortunately, unlike the princesses, Martin believed in magic. He turned round three times, which is a very magical thing to do and then stretching out his hand and pointing at the dragon shouted: 'Begone in the name of the King of Fire.'

Now, the dragon didn't know what this meant, but it sounded terribly frightening and off he ran along a passageway into the depth of the earth and did not dare to come back for many a long day.

The three princesses were hauled to the top of the well by the two servants waiting there and then it was Martin's turn to be hauled up.

It was then that for some reason he remembered the goblin's words. Instead of climbing into the basket himself, he put in a large stone.

He felt pretty stupid as his friends hauled up the stone. What would he say to them when they asked why the stone was in the basket?

But as it turned out, Martin had not been stupid at all. When the basket was half way up the well, his so-called friends let go of the rope and the basket plunged back down.

The two servants then went back to the castle with the princesses, thinking that Martin was dead and that all the glory of finding the princesses would be theirs.

Martin looked around. His life had been saved, but he was trapped in the deep well. What could he do? At last his eyes grew accustomed to the dim light and he saw his friend, the goblin and several other goblins too.

'As you believe in magic, you deserve magical help,' smiled the goblin and he and his friends led Martin along secret passageways out of the mountain and then flew with him back to the royal palace.

He arrived just in time to marry the third princess at the same time as his two friends were marrying the first two. All six of them lived happily ever after, for Martin was kind-hearted and pretended to believe his friends had dropped the basket back down the well accidentally. However, he was very careful not to let them lower him down any wells in future.

# The Steed with Feathers of Flame

Many years ago, in the far distant realms of Russia there lived a fortunate and wealthy king.

His lands were rich with coal and silver and jewels and the people were prosperous and well-behaved.

The king only needed one thing to make his happiness complete and that was a son and heir. At last after many years, the king's wife, Queen Sophie, gave birth to a fine son.

The king and queen were very happy and ordered feasting throughout the land and gifts to be given to everyone. It seemed the whole country was delighted.

But there was one man who was far from pleased. This was the king's cousin, Sir Olaf. Before the new prince had been born, Sir Olaf had been heir to the throne and a very important person. Now the prince was the heir to the throne and Sir Olaf was nothing.

Jealousy consumed the wretched man. The more the baby prince grew strong and good and clever, the more Sir Olaf hated him.

'I must become important again. I *must*!' vowed Sir Olaf and he sat in his room working out a wicked and evil plan.

One dark night he stole the baby prince from his room and rode with him to the high mountains.

'I will leave this little unwanted newcomer where no one will ever find him,' he muttered, 'then once more I shall be the heir to the throne and everyone will come fussing round me and saying nice things to me and giving me presents.'

So this selfish man left baby Prince Arran alone on the mountainside and rode back to the palace and said nothing to anyone.

However, there are more things in distant, lofty mountains than snow and rocks. There are magical, mysterious things. The mountain on which Prince Arran had been left was the home of the Steed with Feathers of Flame.

This magical creature had wings and tail of fiery flame and galloped for ever through the mountain passes, clearing the way for the rushing wind.

The Steed with the Feathers of Flame felt sorry for the helpless baby and, picking it up gently, carried it to the cave where the magical ice maidens lived.

These beautiful girls looked after the little human baby and brought him up healthy and strong and skilful in reading and music and all the things which a young man of those times should know.

Prince Arran was very happy, riding through the mountain passes on the back of

the Steed with the Feathers of Flame, seeing the mountain peaks spread out below him and listening to the stories the wind told as it screamed along behind him.

But if Prince Arran was happy, his bereft parents certainly were not. All they knew was that someone had stolen their child and they were left without their baby and the kingdom had no heir — except Sir Olaf of course.

Sir Olaf was very happy.

Many searches were made for the missing prince, but he was never found, until one day the grieving Queen Sophie heard of a wise woman who lived in the foothills of the high mountains.

Queen Sophie went to see her.

'A lost prince? A lost prince?' cackled the old woman. 'I should be able to find out something about a lost prince. Princes are special. A golden aura shimmers around them wherever they are. Wise women like me can feel its warmth even from afar.'

The woman closed her eyes and sat still for so long that Queen Sophie thought she had gone to sleep. Then the wise woman's eyelids quivered.

'Up in the mountains,' she whispered, 'up in the mountains, in the cave of the ice maidens. In that magical cold cavern where there should be no warmth at all, I can sense warmth. There is a live human being dwelling in that cave. I can see his golden glow dazzling even through my closed eyelids. He must be a prince for sure. Perhaps he is your lost son.'

The wise woman told Queen Sophie how to reach the cave of the ice maidens and the king went up there with a troup of his strongest soldiers.

He knew his son at once because he was the image of himself when he had been a young man. How delighted he was to see him and how pleased the boy was to find his father.

The ice maidens agreed to let Prince Arran go.

'It is right you should be with your own family,' they said, 'but say farewell to the Steed with the Feathers of Flame before you go. He saved your life.'

So Prince Arran went to see the magnificent steed. 'I will always be ready to help you,' neighed the horse, 'pull a feather of flame from my wing. Keep it safely with you always. If you ever need my help toss the feather into water and I shall come thundering to your side and then beware anyone who tries to harm you.'

Feeling grateful for such a promise, Prince Arran went back to his father's palace, where he lived very happily. He married a very agreeable princess and life seemed perfect.

However, Sir Olaf was furious. He had thought the baby prince lost forever years before. He went to the king of the neighbouring kingdom.

'If I tell you all the secrets of the defence of my country, will you send an army to attack it?' he asked. 'Then I will become king and share half the country's wealth with you.'

This was very wicked, but it seemed to Sir Olaf the only way he would become any sort of ruler at all.

The neighbouring king agreed and sent an army with Sir Olaf to attack Prince Arran's father's kingdom. As Sir Olaf knew all the secret ways into the castles and all the positions of the army, the attack was sure to succeed.

The king and Prince Arran saw the attacking army from afar. They heard Sir Olaf was with it and the king's heart quailed. Prince Arran smiled. He drew out the feather of flame and tossed it into a pool. At once the roaring stamping Steed with the Feathers of Flame was at his side.

'Lead the wind to scatter our enemies with the power of a mighty hurricane,' ordered Prince Arran.

And it was done. The enemy army fled back to its own country. Sir Olaf was never heard of again. Knowing that Prince Arran had such a mighty friend, no enemy ever marched against the kingdom again, so Prince Arran and his family lived happily ever after.

# Sleeping Beauty

Once upon a time there lived a king and queen who had been married for many years. They were happy except for one thing. They had no children.

Then at last a little girl was born to them. Princess Rosebud they called her.

The delighted king and queen wanted life to be perfect for their little daughter so they decide to invite fairies to be the baby's god-mothers.

There were thirteen important fairies living in the kingdom. Unfortunately the king and queen had only twelve golden plates. It was well known that fairies like to eat off gold.

'Well,' said the queen, 'we can invite only twelve of the fairies. After all twelve god-mothers will be enough to bring our daughter good health and happiness. We will leave out that bad-tempered red fairy. I have heard she is away on a visit anyway.'

Twelve fairies were invited to the christen-ing feast and one fairy was left out.

At first everything went well. In turn each fairy godmother stepped forward giving the baby princess gifts of such things as goodness, beauty and wisdom.

Eleven godmothers had given their gifts when there was a commotion at the door.

The thirteenth fairy came bursting in. She had come home and heard about the christen-ing. She was furious that she had not been invited.

'So, *I* am not good enough to be a fairy godmother,' she shrieked, looking round the beautiful room with scorn. 'All these other fairies with their silly smiles are able to come here and eat delicious food from golden plates, but *I* may not,' she screeched.

The thirteenth fairy strode forward into the room, the swirl of her fine clothes sending

a cold draught amongst the fearful guests.

'I will teach you miserable mortals to ignore me!' she hissed.

She leaned over the baby's cradle.

'I suppose these other soft-hearted fairies have been making you beautiful and good,' she sneered. 'Well I will be one of your god-mothers and make all their fine gifts in vain.'

The thirteenth fairy looked up at the king and her stare was black and terrifying.

'This is my gift to your daughter,' she said. 'In the fifteenth year of your daughter's life, she will prick her finger with a spindle and she will die.'

The thirteenth godmother stayed long enough to enjoy the dismay of the poor king and queen and then she swept from the room.

The queen wept over the cradle of her baby in despair. Then the last of the twelve fairy godmothers stepped forward.

'I have not given my gift yet,' she said. 'I cannot undo the curse of the last fairy godmother but I can change it a little. When Princess Rosebud pricks her finger on the spindle, she will not die. She and all in the palace will sleep for a hundred years.'

At this the unfortunate king and queen became less distressed. However, the idea of sleeping for one hundred years was not very appealing. The king decided to do everything in his power to save everyone from such a fate.

As the lovely and good Princess Rosebud entered her fifteenth year, the king ordered that all spindles in or near the palace should be burned.

Princess Rosebud was ordered to stay in the palace. It seemed strange to the princess that now she was fifteen she had less freedom.

However, one day Princess Rosebud thought she would amuse herself by walking round every single room in the palace. The old stone building was rambling and huge. The princess was sure there must be many rooms she had never seen at all.

She wandered upstairs and down, from cellar to attic, till she came to a far tower. She was sure she had never even seen it before, let alone explored it. Up the narrow staircase she climbed till she came to a small wooden door. A rusty key was in the lock. The princess turned the key, opened the door and entered the room. Sitting inside was an old woman spinning flax.

'How prettily the spindle whirrs round,' said the princess, stretching out her hand.

As she touched the spindle it pricked her finger. Princess Rosebud fell onto a bed by the window. At first she appeared to be empty of life. Then a little colour returned to her cheeks. She breathed slowly.

She was not dead, but in a deep, deep, sleep.

Throughout the palace everyone else fell asleep where they stood. The king and queen slept by their thrones. The horses slept in the stables, the dogs in the yard, the doves in the dovecot.

The fire stopped flickering in the hearth. The meat set to roast stopped crackling. The cook fell asleep, just as he raised his hand to box the ears of the kitchen boy. The courtiers slept. The guards slept. Even the wind was still.

Round the palace a hedge of briar roses grew up. As the years went by the hedge hid the palace from sight. The tangle of roses twisted so thick that no one could get through.

The folk who lived roundabout grew old and died. At last only one very old man remembered that when he had been a lad there had been tales of how behind the thick hedge of roses slept a beautiful princess in a palace filled with riches.

One day, a handsome prince came to the district and heard the old story. He went to look at the beautiful hedge of roses.

It was one hundred years to the day, since the princess had pricked her finger.

The prince stretched out his hand towards the hedge. Instead of scratching his fingers with thorns as it had scratched everyone else for a hundred years, the hedge pulled back and let the young man through.

He reached the palace. He saw the dogs sleeping in the yard, the horses sleeping in the stables, the doves sleeping in their dovecot. He saw the king and queen by their thrones. He saw the cook with his hand raised to strike the kitchen boy.

He went to the top of the tower and found the princess sleeping. He kissed her and she awoke and fell in love with him.

As the princess stirred, the king and queen awoke. The horses neighed in the stables. The dogs barked in the yard. The doves cooed in the dovecot. The fire burned and the meat crackled. The cook boxed the ears of the kitchen boy. The courtiers rubbed their eyes. The guards marched to and fro. The palace came to life again. Even the wind blew.

The palace gardeners cleared a road through the hedge of roses. How astonished the local folk were to see people from the palace in clothes from a hundred years before.

How astonished the folk from the palace were to see the changes that one hundred years had brought.

The prince married Princess Rosebud and they lived happily ever after. Some things never change.

# King Bunny

Once upon a time, in Scotland, there was a king who had no son and heir. As the king grew old, he wished to choose someone to succeed him to the throne.

'The fairest thing is to hold a competition to choose the bravest and the wisest nobleman,' he said. 'Then there should be no fighting and quarrelling after I die.'

So it was announced and on the appointed day the bravest and the wisest sons of the greatest nobles came to the royal palace.

Everyone gathered to see the great contest and there were gasps of admiration as the fine young men strode by.

But then the gasps of admiration turned to laughter, as last of all walked a rabbit!

'This is ridiculous!' snapped the Lord Chamberlain, giving the rabbit a kick.

But the rabbit spoke up for himself. 'I am of noble rabbit birth,' he said. 'There is nothing in the rules which says a rabbit may not enter the contest.'

The Lord Chamberlain checked the rules and to his fury found the rabbit was right.

'Never mind! Let the rabbit take part,' laughed the king. 'He will never win, so what does it matter?'

So the various tests went ahead and to everyone's surprise the rabbit did very well and so, of course, did many of the fine young men.

It was when the running race took place that the trouble really came. The rabbit, being small and swift outran all except two of the young men. The king began to frown.

Next came the dagger fight and everyone started to laugh again. How could a tiny rabbit with a dagger the size of a needle ever defeat two young men with daggers like tigers' teeth?

Again the rabbit surprised everyone. He dashed forward quickly and nipped one young man on the toe and the other on the ankle. They cried out in anguish.

He had drawn first blood. He was the winner.

Only the test of book learning remained. Surely no rabbit could pass this test? The king smiled at the young man who was second behind the rabbit.

'You will surely be king,' he said.

But the rabbit answered every question put to him by the wise men. He was learned and wise. There was no help for it. He had to be declared heir to the throne.

The announcement was made and everyone gasped in horror. A rabbit for king!

Then there was a clap of thunder as had never been heard before. The skies darkened. Lightning flashed. The rabbit turned into a fine young prince. He had been under a wicked spell, but now he was free and in course of time he did become king and he was called King Bunny.

# The Golden Apples

In ancient Greece there lived a king called Jason. Those were warlike days and a small kingdom needed a strong soldier to lead it.

Jason longed for a son, whom he could teach the arts of war and who could defend the kingdom when Jason became old.

However even kings do not always get what

they want in this life. When the queen gave birth to a child, it was a daughter. King Jason was terribly disappointed and then he fell into a rage.

'Why are the gods laughing at me by sending me a daughter, when I need a son so much?' he shouted.

He ordered his servants to take the little girl, Atalanta, and leave her out on the mountainside to perish.

This was done. As darkness fell, the little baby was left alone in the forest on the mountains, but the baby did not die.

A big brown bear was ambling back to its lair when it heard the baby crying. To the bear it seemed like the wailing of a bear cub. The big shambling creature picked up the baby and took her back to its cave. It fed her and kept her warm and for week after week the little mite went on living and growing stronger.

The baby became a toddler and the toddler became a strong, wild little creature, running with the big bear and learning all the ways of nature.

Meanwhile King Jason was regretting his rash action. Girl or not, the baby was his own flesh and blood. He sent his soldiers to comb the forest and after many months they found a wild creature with human form running through the mountain passes. The child was the image of her father King Jason. This must be Atalanta.

The little girl was captured and taken back to the palace to be brought up as a proper human child.

Atalanta was clever. She soon learned to speak and to adapt to the way of life in the palace, but she never forgot her wild life in the forest. She loved animals and the woodlands. Most of all she loved running free.

As she grew older it became clear that Atalanta was amongst the fastest runners who had ever lived, man or woman.

At last the time came when Atalanta should marry. The thought of settling down and giving up her freedom did not appeal to her.

'I will only marry a man who can run faster than I can,' she said to King Jason.

As Atalanta was such a swift runner, it seemed that she would never marry and this was the way she liked things to be.

Several young men asked for Atalanta's hand and races were arranged in front of all the nobility in the kingdom. Atalanta always won.

Then the son of the Sea God, a strong and handsome young man called Hippomenes, saw Atalanta running along the sea shore. At once he wished to marry her.

He visited King Jason and learned of the conditions for any marriage with Atalanta. He agreed to run a race and a time and place was arranged.

Now Hippomenes could run swiftly, but he knew that it would be difficult to beat Atalanta. He was also a clever young man.

'I must use cunning.as well as strength,' he thought and he went to visit the goddess Aphrodite.

Hippomenes bowed low before Aphrodite and presented her with a lovely necklace of pearls made in the kingdom of his father the Sea God.

'Help me, oh beautiful Aphrodite, goddess of love,' he begged.

Aphrodite was delighted with the necklace and pleased with the young man's polite manner.

'How can I aid you?' she asked.

Hippomenes explained that he wished to marry Atalanta, but that first he had to out-run her in a race.

'Do not worry about how swiftly you can race,' smiled Aphrodite. 'Take these three golden apples. Use them as I tell you and Atalanta will never out-run you.'

Aphrodite handed Hippomenes three heavy, glowing, beautifully carved solid gold apples and told him how he should use them.

The day of the race arrived. King Jason and all the nobles gathered to watch. Atalanta and Hippomenes stood together at the starting line.

Atalanta looked into Hippomenes' eyes. For the first time she was in love, but still her pride made her want to win the race. She could not bear to think that anyone was fleeter than she.

The race started and it was clear that Atalanta could run faster than Hippomenes. His very strength made him heavier than the girl who seemed to blow across the grass like thistledown.

Remembering Aphrodite's instructions, Hippomenes dropped the first apple. Its lovely golden gleam caught Atalanta's eye. She stooped to pick it up and gasped at its beauty. How could she leave such a lovely thing lying on the ground?

By this time Hippomenes was well ahead, but so swiftly could Atalanta run that she soon drew level.

Hippomenes dropped another apple. Again Atalanta stopped to pick it up. This apple was even more beautiful than the other. She must keep both of them. She clutched them to her and went on running. However the apples were very heavy and carrying them made Atalanta's movements awkward. She could not catch up with Hippomenes until the finishing post. Then, just as she seemed to be about to surge ahead of him, the young man threw down the last apple.

Atalanta bent to pick it up and the race was lost to her. Hippomenes ran past the winning post. Atalanta would have to marry him.

However, as Atalanta was now in love with Hippomenes, she was happy to get married. King Jason was pleased with his clever and strong son-in-law and finally everyone was content.

# Michael and the Mighty Men

Once, long ago, there was a young fellow called Michael, who lived in a little village in the country.

The village was quite pleasant and Michael had enough to eat and enough money to buy himself neat working clothes, but this didn't seem quite enough.

'I want to be rich,' thought Michael. 'I want to eat fine food from painted china plates and drink wine from golden goblets. I want to live in a grand house, with comfortable chairs and a view from the windows.'

Michael looked round his humble, little village.

'I shall never find such things here,' he decided and packing some food and what little money he had, Michael set out to make his fortune. After a while, Michael found

himself walking along the edge of a forest and here an amazing sight met his eyes.

A huge man was felling trees with one blow of his axe and then picking up the trees and carrying them without any help at all to the sawmill.

Michael had never seen such strength.

'You are wasting your time here,' he said to the strong man. 'Come with me to find a place where you can use your strength to make a fortune.'

The strong man agreed and he walked with Michael along the highway. They hadn't gone far before they saw a hunter aiming his gun. He seemed to be about to shoot a horse in the next field.

'Why are you shooting that horse?' asked Michael in surprise. 'He is doing no harm and he looks healthy enough.'

'I am not going to shoot the horse,' replied the hunter. 'Watch.'

He finished taking aim, fired the gun and when Michael and the strong man went over to the horse, they found that the hunter had shot a wasp which had been annoying the horse.

'What wonderful markmanship!' gasped Michael. He turned to the hunter. 'You are wasted in a small place like this,' he said. 'Why don't you come with us and seek your fortune in a big place where you can make a famous man of yourself?'

The marksman agreed and set off along the highway with Michael and the strong man.

After a while, the three of them came to a windmill. The sails of the windmill were racing round. They were turning faster than any sails the three men had ever seen before.

'Perhaps there is some sort of engine inside the mill,' said Michael. The three friends went inside, but no engine was to be seen. It was all very puzzling, but the three friends had better things to worry about than the sails of windmills and they went on their way.

However on a little hill at the side of the road, they saw a jolly-looking fellow sitting blowing gently through his lips. Michael and the strong man and the hunter turned their heads and saw that the man was blowing in the direction of the windmill.

It was his gentle blowing which was turning the mighty windmill so swiftly!

The jolly fellow saw Michael and the strong man and the hunter staring at him.

'This is nothing,' he smiled. 'If I really blow hard, I can make a hurricane sweep across the land, flattening everything before it.'

'How marvellous!' gasped Michael. 'However don't try it just at the moment, will you! Why don't you walk along with us instead? We are all off to find some big city where we can make our fortunes. A gift like yours must be very useful to someone. Why don't you come with us and seek your fortune too?'

The man stood up at once.

'I will,' he smiled. 'I have always wanted to see the great big world, but going adventuring alone can be dangerous. If I travel with three such companions as you, I am sure I shall be quite safe.'

The four companions strode along the road, sheltering in barns at night, keeping warm with wood collected by the strong man and eating food found by the hunter.

After a few more days the four friends saw a man sitting outside a cottage with his legs tied together. He looked quite cheerful and not at all distressed by his condition.

'Good friend, why are your legs tied together like that?' asked Michael.

The man, who was tall and thin, with very long legs, smiled.

'I am not a prisoner, as you might think,' he said. 'I am a very fast runner. If my legs were untied they would start running so fast that in the twinkling of an eye I should be ten miles away. I tie my legs together when I want to stay at home and have a rest.'

'Well,' thought Michael, 'a fellow who can run as fast as that would be very useful to a king who wanted to send important messages to all parts of his realm. He should come with us, too.'

Michael told the tall man the wonderful things his mighty companions could do and at once the tall man agreed to join them.

He slackened the ropes round his legs enough to allow him to walk with his new friends and then he said: 'I have a friend with a very unusual gift. I think he should join us on our quest for riches.'

He took Michael and the strong man and the hunter and the jolly fellow who could blow hard to visit a man who sat in front of a hot fire and who had a thick hat pulled down over one ear.

The only thing remarkable about this man seemed to be the odd way he wore his hat.

'Oh, I have to wear my hat this way,' he explained, 'if I uncovered this ear, it would send out a blast of cold air, icy enough to freeze the world.'

'My word!' gasped Michael. 'Well, don't do it just at the moment, but come along with us. A gift like that might be very useful to someone.'

So Michael went on his way with now five mighty men at his side.

At last they came to a great palace in-habited by a rich and powerful king, just the sort of man who might pay well for their services.

They asked at the palace gate if the king needed anything and learned that he required nothing. However they also learned that he had a daughter who could run very fast. The king had offered the princess's hand to any-one who could beat her in a race.

This was only done to give the king and the courtiers entertainment. The princess ran so fast no one ever beat her. She and the king and the lords and ladies just laughed at the poor fellow who came puffing along behind her.

Thinking that good fortune had come to them at last, Michael asked if his tall friend could race against the princess. It was arran-ged. The tall man untied the rope from his legs and in a twinkling was far ahead of the girl. However he was over-confident and lay down for a rest before he reached the winning post.

The princess was indeed a swift runner and even though she paused for a drink, she over-took the tall man and seemed about to win.

Michael and the others were in despair.

'Wake up! Wake up!' they shouted, but they were too far away for the tall man to hear them.

Then the hunter picked up his gun. He took careful aim and fired. He hit a tuft of grass just by the tall thin man's ear. He woke with a start, saw what was happening and with a flash of flying legs was at the winning post just before the princess.

Now he should have married the princess and shared his wealth with his companions.

However, this did not happen.

The king did not want his daughter to marry some vagabond and the princess certainly had no intentions of doing so.

'I am going to marry a prince, as befits my station,' she said to her father. 'You made the arrangement for this silly race. Now you undo it all and get rid of that wretched man and his tiresome friends.'

'Of course, of course, my dear,' replied the king. 'Leave it all to me.'

He invited Michael and his friends to come and stay at the palace, but instead of showing them into comfortable bedrooms, as they had expected, he ushered them into an iron room and locked the door behind them.

Then he ordered his servants to build a fire under the room.

'When they got hot enough they will agree to anything,' he smiled, 'and I will make that tall man say he doesn't want to marry the princess after all.'

The fire roared up and the iron room became unbearably hot.

'We shall have to give in,' gasped Michael, 'we cannot stay here.'

'Oh yes we can,' smiled the man with the hat on the side of his head.

The man took off his hat and an icy blast swirled all round the red-hot iron room. At once the metal cooled and the friends were able to sit quite comfortably until the amazed king opened the door.

Then the king had another idea.

'If I give you a sackful of gold, will you go away?' he asked.

Michael and his friends agreed. After all they wanted to make their fortunes and the thin man would just as soon marry his sweetheart back home as the princess.

'But may we use our own sack?' asked Michael, and the king agreed.

He was rather upset when he saw Michael bring a simply enormous sack, but the king thought:

'Even if they fill that sack, they will never be able to carry it. They will have to empty some of the gold out again, so I shall not lose much money.'

However, when the enormous sack was full, the strong man put it on his back and carried it away easily. The king was furious and sent his army to bring the gold back.

Then the jolly man who had been blowing the sails of the windmill round blew a hurricane and scattered the king's armies. So Michael and his friends walked away with the gold and lived in comfort for ever after.

113

# Springtime Revels

Sandra and Sally were two very nice, good little girls who lived with their mummy and daddy in a house near a park.

Every afternoon, unless the weather was too bad, Mummy would take Sandra and Sally to feed the ducks on the lake in the park.

After they had fed the ducks and if there was no shopping to be done, Mummy would stay in the park so that the two little girls could play.

Sandra and Sally would play chase or skipping or pretending to be mummies with babies, but they were always careful not to tread on any flowers and they certainly never dropped any rubbish.

They were careful to keep the park tidy because they were good little girls. They never thought that anyone was noticing *how* good they were being.

One evening in the springtime, Sandra and Sally and Mummy had been to the park as usual and as usual they had gone home and had tea and the children had been bathed by Mummy. Then, as usual, they stayed up just long enough to say hallo to Daddy when he came home. And then as usual the children went to bed, looked at their books for a while and then, just as usual, Mummy put out the lights and the children went to sleep.

But in those few minutes after the light went out and when Sandra and Sally's eyes were growing accustomed to the dark and beginning to make out the shape of the windows and to see the curtains moving in the breeze from the small window Mummy always left open for fresh air — then something very unusual happened.

The curtains fluttered and tweaked apart.

There was a flash of silvery light and a green elf with sparkling wings was standing in the room.

'My name is Peasblossom,' he said, 'and I have come to invite you to some revels.'

'What are revels?' asked Sandra.

'Well, it's like a party,' explained Peasblossom. 'Everyone dresses up and then there is a lot of jolly chatting and dancing.'

Even as Peasblossom was speaking, the walls of the bedroom were melting away and the two girls found themselves back in the park.

Strangely it wasn't dark, as it had been in their bedroom. A glorious golden light lit up everything. The girls were no longer wearing their nightdresses. They were in the prettiest dresses made of tiny flowers. They found themselves dancing as light as thistledown with the laughing elves and fairies.

One beautiful young lady sat watching them. 'I am the Spirit of Spring,' she smiled. 'I have invited you to this revel because you are such good girls.'

After lots of dancing and laughter Sandra and Sally woke up in their own beds. And do you know, Mummy said they had been dreaming. What an idea!

# The Snow Maidens

At the foot of a mighty mountain yawned a dark, fearsome cavern. The air inside was stale and sour. No animal lived there, not even a mouse. No one knew how deep it was. No one dared to go in to find out. All anyone in the nearby village knew was that it was wise to stay away from the cavern.

Then one springtime everyone learned why the cavern was such a fearsome place and why all the old wives' tales said that no one should go near it.

As dawn was lighting the sky on the first day of spring a terrible thundering roar raced from the cavern. The ground shook and a mighty dragon came storming forth.

His fiery breath burned the crops and the woodlands and his huge jaws ate every living creature which crossed his path.

The terrified villagers spoke to the oldest wise woman in the region.

'My grandmother told me about that dragon,' she said, 'but I did not believe her. I thought it was a story to frighten me into behaving myself. The story is that the dragon sleeps in the depths of that cavern and wakes every hundred years. It will rampage across the countryside until it has eaten its fill and then it will sleep for another hundred years.'

The villagers were horrified, but what could they do?

It was then that a wandering minstrel passed through the district. He was a fine musician and folk gathered to listen to his songs to try to take their minds of their troubles.

It so happened that one of the farmers had two beautiful daughters. Their skins were so clear and fair that they were called the Snow Maidens. These girls liked to sing, but of course normally there wasn't much time for singing on a busy farm.

However as the minstrel was there to lead them, the girls did sing, and sang as they had never sung before.

The minstrel smiled at the village folk.

'Your troubles are over,' he said. 'These girls have the most beautiful voices I have ever heard. Send them to sing lullabies to the dragon and it will fall into another hundred years' sleep.'

The brave girls did as the minstrel said. The dragon's roars turned to snores. It crept back into the depths of the cave. The village was saved, thanks to the Snow Maidens.

# The
# Treasure Casket

Once upon a time, there was a beautiful princess. Her name was Silver Moon. Silver Moon lived with her father, the King of China, in a glittering crystal palace at the side of the deep blue sea. Two gnomes named Pik and Pok were her best friends.

Silver Moon was in love with a prince from far-away in India. The prince was tall, handsome, clever, rich and also a brave soldier, all of which should have been quite enough to make him the right sort of man to be the husband of Silver Moon.

However, King Silver Locks, the father of Princess Silver Moon, was very fussy.

'We must see if Prince Amon is kind and generous,' he said to Silver Moon. 'It is no use for you to have a rich husband if he does not share his riches with you.'

So it was arranged that Princess Amon should come on a visit.

'We shall watch how he behaves,' said King Silver Locks. 'If he gives presents to the man who has cooked his food and the woman who has washed his clothes, as well as the usual presents he is expected to give to you and to me, then we shall know that he is truly generous.'

A golden ship with sails the colour of the setting sun was sent across the rolling blue sea to bring Prince Amon to the crystal palace on the cliff tops. It was away for many a long day, but at last it returned. Princess Silver Moon watched its arrival from the cliff tops.

However, suddenly the wind changed. It swept the beautiful ship back out to sea. There was nothing the captain could do. Princess Silver Moon was upset. Now it could be days before the prince could come ashore. Then the princess thought of her own boat. It was made from a huge sea shell and was pulled by two black swans.

'My shell boat does not need the wind to blow it along,' said Silver Moon. 'The swans can pull it along no matter which way the wind blows.'

Princess Silver Moon ordered the two gnomes Pik and Pok to take the shell boat out to the big ship and bring Prince Amon quickly to shore. This the two gnomes did.

'Come with us,' they called to Prince Amon. 'The black swans will pull us safely to the shore. The captain can follow in the ship, when the wind changes.'

'Very well,' called Prince Amon, 'but I

must bring one thing with me — the casket containing my treasure.'

Prince Amon climbed down the side of the swaying golden ship and soon he was skimming over the waves in the shell boat pulled by the black swans.

'I had to bring this casket with me,' he said. 'In it are my presents to Princess Silver Moon and her father, King Silver Locks and also all the other presents I have brought for everyone in the palace.'

Then Prince Amon turned to look towards the shore to try to catch a first glimpse of Princess Silver Moon. Unfortunately Pik and Pok were very inquisitive. They wanted to look at the presents. While Prince Amon's back was turned they balanced the casket on the side of the boat where the light was bright and they opened it. They rummaged about inside the casket trying to decide which presents they would like for themselves. Of course, in their haste they were careless and they dropped the casket over the side of the boat into the sea.

This was dreadful. If Prince Amon arrived without presents, he would look very mean, whatever excuses he gave.

'We must ask Princess Pearl, the mermaid to help us,' gasped Pik. He pulled a golden whistle from his pocket and blew a call from it down into the sea. Soon there was a swirl of golden hair and a mermaid with a face as pale as a pearl swam to the surface. Pik explained what had happened and begged the mermaid to bring back the casket.

'If it contains so many beautiful things I might keep it for myself,' replied Princess Pearl, the mermaid. 'Why should I give it back to you?'

Pik thought hard. 'Because if you do, I will give you my share of the palace chocolate cake for a month,' he smiled.

Now there are plenty of jewels in the sea, but very little chocolate cake, so Princess Pearl agreed.

The casket was given back, Prince Amon gave everyone wonderful presents and he was allowed to marry the Princess Silver Moon.

Everyone was happy, especially the mermaid, Princess Pearl, who sat on the rocks at the foot of the cliffs eating chocolate cake every afternoon for a happy month.

# The Country Boy

Once upon a time, there was a very simple young lad, who lived in the country. His name was Andrew. Andrew was not worldly wise, that is to say he did not always do what was in his own best interest.

For instance, he was out one cold day when he saw a sheep standing out in a field.

'That poor sheep must be cold,' thought kind Andrew and taking off his jacket, he put it round the sheep.

As soon as Andrew reached home, his mother asked him where his jacket had gone. Andrew told her what he had done. His mother was furious.

'Fetch your jacket at once,' she shouted. 'Sheep are made to live outdoors in the cold. They don't need human clothes.'

Andrew ran back to fetch his jacket and at the roadside he found a box of gold pieces.

'This must be robbers' gold,' he thought. 'It is dishonest money. I must not have anything to do with it.'

He threw it into the river.

Again he told his mother what he had done and again she was furious.

'We could have done with that money,' she shrieked. 'And even if we had not kept it all, you could have got a reward by taking it to its rightful owner.'

Andrew felt very foolish.

Tired of having such a stupid boy about the house, Andrew's mother sent him to work for a merchant in the nearest town.

Andrew did well in the merchant's house. He did exactly as he was told and everyone liked him.

Then the day came when the merchant went on a foreign voyage. He asked everyone in his house what they would like brought back from the trip.

Being just a country boy, Andrew did not know much about foreign lands. He gave the merchant a coin from his wages.

'Buy me anything you think I will like,' he said.

So the merchant went about his business, but he could find nothing nice to buy with Andrew's coin. Then one day, just as his ship was leaving a foreign harbour, the merchant saw an old woman with a cat. 'Andrew would like a cat as a pet,' thought the merchant. He bought the cat with Andrew's coin.

The cat stayed with the merchant quite happily and then the day came when the ship called in at yet another strange port. The merchant did some good business and then was invited out to dinner by his new foreign friends.

No sooner had they all sat down to the table and the food been put in front of them than a swarm of mice raced out from their holes and snatched at the food. They ran squeaking over the merchant's feet and up his legs and leapt on to the table, their dirty little paws treading over his spoon and across his plate.

It was quite unpleasant. The merchant didn't feel like eating even such food as was left to him.

His foreign friends sighed: 'We do not like the mice either, but what can we do?' they said.

'I know what you can do,' replied the

merchant. He sent for his cat from the ship and set it on to the mice. In a few days there was not a mouse left in the place.

Everyone was so pleased they gave the merchant a bag of gold in reward. When he reached home the merchant gave Andrew the bag of gold and the cat — at which Andrew was very pleased.

For a simple country boy, he felt he had done very well.

# The Donkey Who Thought He Was Clever

Donald the donkey had worked for the same master for many years. Every week they would leave their little farm to go to market in the neighbouring town. The master, Farmer Giles, would sell his goods, have a jolly lunch with his farmer friends, buy something he needed himself and then he would drive back to the farm.

However on the return journey, Farmer Giles did not do much driving. He was tired after his day out and he would usually doze and let Donald the donkey make his own way home.

Fortunately, as Donald had made the same journey for many years, he did know the way home. Year in, year out, the weekly trip to market took place with no trouble.

Then Donald the donkey fell to thinking. 'Farmer Giles never notices the way we go home,' he thought. 'If I crossed the river further up, instead of walking all the way to that ford, I should save my poor old hooves at least two miles trotting.'

Crossing the river in a different place seemed a very clever idea and Donald decided to do it. Into the river went Donald the donkey, pulling the cart and the dozing Farmer Giles after him. The river was much deeper here, which was why Farmer Giles liked to go further along to cross by the ford.

Still Donald went on scrambling his way forward. The river water washed all through the contents of the cart, which as it happened was salt! Salt is dissolved in water and by the

time they reached the far side of the river, most of the salt had gone.

Donald was delighted to feel how light the cart had become. From then on, dragging the cart was much easier. He decided that crossing the river in a different place was a fine idea and that he would do it the next week.

Farmer Giles was puzzled by the missing salt, but didn't guess the real reason for it.

The next week Farmer Giles and Donald the donkey went to market as usual. Farmer Giles had a fine day out and, on the way home, he dozed in the cart and let Donald make his own way.

Feeling very clever Donald plunged into the river at the new crossing place. What a terrible mistake he was making. This week instead of being filled with salt, the cart was filled with sponges!

Sponges soak up water and become much heavier when they are wet.

Poor Donald!

The cart was so heavy when the donkey reached the far bank that he could not pull his load out of the water.

Who knows what would have happened if all the splashing and scrambling had not woken Farmer Giles. At once he tossed the heavy sponges on to the bank until the cart was light enough for Donald to pull out of the river.

So all ended safely, but Donald never tried to be clever and think for himself again!

# The Wishing~Trout

Once a poor peasant lived in a small hut near a mountainside. He grew enough to eat on his little plot of land and sometimes was lucky enough to catch fish in a mountain stream.

One day he caught a fine speckled trout in the stream. The peasant was pleased. He and his wife enjoyed a nice supper of fried trout.

However the trout spoke to him and said:

'Please throw me back into the stream. You will not regret your kindness. If you spare my life, you will only have to return to the bank of this stream and I will grant any wish you ask.'

The peasant threw the trout back into the stream and went home and told his wife what he had done. She was cross.

'You are stupid,' she grumbled, 'now we shall have to eat warmed up turnip pie for supper, when we could have been enjoying fried trout. And if that trout is so clever and can grant wishes, why haven't you wished for something?'

The truth was the wife did not believe the story at all. She thought her husband had dropped the trout back into the water by accident and was now making excuses.

'I tell you that trout really did talk,' protested the peasant. To prove his words, he went back to the side of the stream and wished.

'Instead of my humble hut, I should like a nice farmhouse with stables and pigsties and plenty of land well planted with potatoes and carrots and fruit trees,' he said.

The trout poked his head out of the water.

'I will grant your wish, as I promised,' he said, 'and I hope your wife will be pleased.'

The peasant hurried home and found the lovely farm waiting for him. He was very happy and so was his wife — at first.

After a while, the wife said: 'This farm is all very well, but if we can have what we like, why don't we have a fine castle?'

The peasant went back to the side of the stream and called to the trout.

'I wish for a castle,' he said, 'and fine dresses for my wife and lots of servants to do the work.'

'I will grant your wish and I hope your wife will be pleased,' replied the fish.

When the peasant went home he found the wonderful castle waiting. He and his wife moved in at once. After a while his wife said:

'This castle is all very well, but managing it is a lot of work and worry. Why don't you go back to that fish and say that we want — Paradise. We're sure to be content there.'

The peasant went back to the side of the stream and asked the trout to give them Paradise to live in.

'Very well,' agreed the fish. 'This is the last wish and I hope your wife will be pleased.'

How astonished the peasant was when he returned home to find all the grand things gone and only his little hut and small piece of land waiting for him.

The trout had decided that Paradise for the peasant and his wife was their old simple life. Let us hope they were happy with it.

# The Legend of the Snows

At once he asked the princess if she would like to marry him.

'Yes,' she whispered, not daring to give any other reply.

'Good,' replied King Black Flame.

'We shall be married within the month.'

Princess Snow was dismayed. How could so much be happening so quickly?

'Oh no,' she gasped.

'I don't want to get married in a month,' protested Princess Snow. 'It will still be winter. Everything will be frozen. The trees will be bare, the sky will be grey, the rivers and the lakes will be icy. There won't be any flowers. We must wait till the springtime when everything will be so much nicer. The meadows will be a carpet of blossoms, the

Old King Silver-beard had a beautiful daughter. He never stopped admiring her. He was always saying to his wife, the queen, 'My goodness! We shall never find anyone good enough to marry our daughter, Snow.'

Snow was the lovely girl's name.

Princess Snow herself didn't give marriage a thought. She was far too happy at the palace to want to change things.

However, one day, King Black Flame, the powerful ruler of the neighbouring kingdom, came to the palace on an official visit.

He was an overwhelming person to meet. He was dark and strong and clever and commanding in his manner.

beard. 'It is only right he should think about work and not bother with flowers and pretty speeches.'

Princess Snow burst into tears and at once her father was sorry. 'We will do our best to make things nice with flowers from the palace hot-houses,' he said.

The day of the wedding arrived. Princess Snow's fiancé, King Black Flame, came to the palace surrounded by tough soldiers and haughty proud dukes and palace dignitaries. The weather was cold. The sky was grey. There was not a flower in the meadow nor a leaf on a tree.

However King Black Flame had brought some magnificent presents for his bride. There were yards of rich material bought from merchants who had travelled to the furthest Eastern countries. There were sapphires and diamonds and beautifully made gold and silver necklaces and bracelets.

'Well, this really is very nice,' thought Princess Snow.

However she did wish that her intended husband could sit and whisper sweet nothings to her, instead of attending to business all the time.

'You do love me, don't you?' she whispered to King Black Flame.

'Oh yes, yes,' he muttered, 'but I hope you won't expect a lot of pretty speechifying when you get back to my kingdom. My future sub-

pine trees will be perfuming the woodlands. The birds will be singing.'

Her fiancé, the king, was impatient. 'That talk is all very well,' he shrugged, 'but official duties mean we must marry within the month and that is all there is to say about it.'

He went back to his kingdom to make arrangements for the marriage.

Princess Snow was vexed. If her fiancé could have been a little more poetic and a little less businesslike, she would have been better pleased.

She complained about it to her parents, but her father King Silver-beard took the other king's part.

'King Black Flame has a large kingdom bordered by many enemies,' said King Silver-

jects expect me to bring back a dignified queen, not a silly girl.'

At those words poor Princess Snow thought her heart would become as cold as the winter landscape outside the window.

She was unhappy all through the wedding ceremony and afterwards when everyone was congratulating her, she could hardly restrain her tears.

The moment the wedding feast and the speeches were over, King Black Flame turned to his new wife.

'Well, we're married now,' he said, 'let's be on our way back to my kingdom. I can't stay here any longer. Affairs of state are waiting.'

Snow looked deep into his eyes, hoping for some understanding.

'I don't want to leave all my beautiful wedding flowers. Couldn't they be put to decorate our carriage? And could the carriage be pulled by white horses? It *is* our wedding journey.'

'I can't be bothered with rubbish like that,' said the king. 'It's time to go.'

Snow was very upset, but she walked with her new husband through the palace rooms of her happy childhood. Before they could reach their carriage a servant stopped them. 'Your majesties, you will not be able to leave,' he said. 'An amazing thing is happening. Tiny flakes like white butterflies are falling from the skies. They are covering the fields and blocking the roads.'

For the first time ever, what we call snow had fallen. The countryside looked beautiful, in a different way, as beautiful as it did in summer. Even King Black Flame forgot affairs of state and gasped at its beauty. From that moment he started noticing the more poetic things of life. Snow was happy and the little flakes of white were called after her, as they fell on her wedding day.

# Tiny Tom

Far away in Russia there once lived a very small man called Tiny Tom. As he was so small, he had learned to be quite cunning. He had to outdo the bigger folk by using his wits.

Another thing about Tiny Tom was that he always slept very soundly. He had to run so fast with his little legs, just to keep up with normal sized people, that he was always exhausted!

One day Tiny Tom had been out working. This had made him so tired that on the way home he had a sleep on a leaf at the side of the road. It happened also that day that the ruler of Russia, the Czar, was out hunting with some of his men. The Czar was amazed when he saw Tiny Tom sleeping on the leaf. He tried to wake him up, but Tom was so deeply asleep that he wouldn't wake.

Now, in Russia, if the Czar wanted someone to wake up, they had to wake! The Czar told all his men to fire their guns at once.

'That should wake the stubborn little fellow up,' he grunted.

'What on earth is all the noise about?' gasped Tom, jumping up. 'What a stupid thing to do to fire all those guns at once.'

Of course he didn't realize he was talking to the Czar. When he did see who was standing in front of him, he bowed low and asked how he could be of service.

'A little thing like you be of service?' laughed the Czar. 'Why, you must be quite useless.'

'I could catch a bear,' he claimed, 'which is more than many normal-sized men can do.'

'Catch a bear!' jeered the Czar. 'I'll believe it when I see it.'

However the Czar was interested in what the cheeky little fellow could do and it was arranged that the next day there should be a bear hunt.

Tiny Tom filled his pockets with small stones and went to meet the Czar and his hunters as arranged. The hunters spread out in the forest banging sticks and shouting. Before long, a bear, upset and angry at all the noise ran out into the clearing where Tom and the Czar were waiting.

'Now is your chance,' grinned the Czar.

However Tom knew what he was doing. He ran ahead of the bear and behind it and teased it from behind leaves and stones until the bear was quite confused and worn out. All the while Tom was enticing the bear towards an old hut in the forest.

The tired bear lay down to have a rest. At once Tom tormented it by throwing the tiny stones at its nose. In a rage, the bear lumbered up and leapt at Tom. Tom was cleverly standing in front of the open door of the hut. As Tom was so tiny, the bear missed him completely and landed in the hut. Tom slammed the door shut and the bear was caught.

'Bravo!' shouted the Czar and gave Tom a bag of gold for amusing him so well.

133

# The Magic Ruby

Long ago in ancient Persia, there lived a powerful and terrifying Shah. His riches were immense and the world trembled before his armies. His wisdom had made his country prosperous and his love of beautiful things meant that his capital city was elegant to behold. Then, one day it befell that a pilgrim walked towards this fine city. This pilgrim had nothing but the ragged clothes on his back and he walked slowly because his feet were bruised and tired. The man was hungry and was thinking of nothing but where his next crust of bread might come from, when he saw something shining in the dust of the road. It was a red stone, which glowed with a brilliant light. He bent forward and picked it up, thinking it might be of some use, but not realizing that fate had at last thrown good fortune in his path.

When he reached the capital city, the pilgrim made his way to the palace of the

Shah, rightly thinking that this might be a good place to sell the red stone. He asked one of the palace guards if he might be permitted to speak to the royal cook. The cook was quite an important man in charge of an army of kitchen hands.

'Why do you want to see me, pilgrim?' asked the cook, who was quite a good sort of fellow and patient enough to talk to a poor beggar.

'I have found a pretty red stone,' said the pilgrim. 'Will you take it in exchange for a meal? Just one meal — that is all I ask.'

He held out the shiny stone and showed it to the cook. The cook took it and turned it over and then turned it again and looked at it closely.

Actually he knew quite a bit about precious stones and he spoke seriously to the pilgrim.

'This stone is worth more than one meal,' he said. 'I'm pretty sure my master, the Shah, would give you a good price for it. Why don't you try him?'

The pilgrim was amazed. He had not guessed the stone was so valuable. But getting in to speak to the Shah was difficult and risky. The Shah was not always in a good mood.

However, the Shah was already very

135

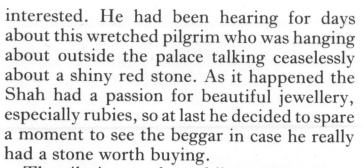

interested. He had been hearing for days about this wretched pilgrim who was hanging about outside the palace talking ceaselessly about a shiny red stone. As it happened the Shah had a passion for beautiful jewellery, especially rubies, so at last he decided to spare a moment to see the beggar in case he really had a stone worth buying.

The pilgrim stood trembling in front of the magnificent throne, bowed to the ground and then presented the red stone to the Shah.

The Shah looked at it with his mouth agape. Such an attitude was not in accord with the dignity of his position. He hastily pulled himself together. He did not attempt to argue over the value of the gem — such ways are not worthy of grand monarchs — he gave the pilgrim a large bag of gold and took the ruby and shut it carefully away in a jewel box.

Well pleased, the pilgrim withdrew from the presence of the Shah who, busy with affairs of state, gave no more thought to the jewel. It was at first simply added to his great collection of gems.

However, after a while the Shah thought he would get out the new jewel and admire it. He went to his treasure house and opened the box. Imagine his amazement when out stepped a young man of surpassing beauty. A moment later, the ruby completely vanished without trace.

'Where have you come from?' asked the Shah, when at last he was able to speak.

'I am the Prince of Rubies,' replied the

young man with a smile,' and for the moment that is all I can tell you.'

The Shah felt his blood boiling in his veins. His valuable ruby had disappeared and instead here was this young man sprung from nowhere, refusing to answer a very reasonable question. He would take the smile from his face.

'Very well then,' said the Shah. 'I'm sure I don't want to know anything out of place.' He deceitfully put on a friendly tone and went on. 'Please allow me to give you an outfit suitable to your rank and a sword of gold and in return do you think I could ask you to do me a small service?'

This is what the cunning fellow was about: For some time a huge dragon had been prowling round the capital city. He had killed so many of the Shah's subjects that the affair had become boring and the Shah had sent officers of the royal guard to get rid of the dragon.

However that plan hadn't worked out very brilliantly and the Shah didn't care to talk about it. Suffice it to say that the dragon was still on the prowl and the Shah had had to make a pact with him to keep him reasonably quiet.

Every month the Shah sent a young man of the best family for the dragon to eat. Naturally the Shah wanted to be rid of the whole embarrassing situation. He had promised to give his daughter in marriage to any hero who could kill the dragon.

However, the way things were going, it seemed that Fatima, the joy of the Shah's life, would die an old maid, for, with a great lack of understanding of the right way to behave, the dragon kept killing every young man who came before him.

'Would you like to kill a dragon for me?' the Shah asked the Prince of Rubies.

'Certainly,' replied the prince. 'I should be delighted.'

'If you win, you may marry my daughter, Fatima, the light of my life,' smiled the Shah.

Thus it was that the Prince of Rubies donned a suit of glittering armour and took the road to the little wood where the dragon came to eat his victims. Everything was quiet. The prince sat down against a large tree and time went by.

Nothing happened for so long that the prince even dozed a little in the warm sun.

Then, suddenly, there was the most terrifying noise and the dragon burst from the forest. It was huge and ugly; fire came from its eyes and smoke from its nostrils. But the prince did not hesitate. He leapt to his feet, drew his sword, strode towards the dragon and a tremendous battle followed. For its size the dragon was amazingly agile but, quick as it was, the prince was quicker. For half-a-day they fought but at last the prince was victorious and the dragon lay at his feet.

The prince took the dragon's head back to the Shah and he was married to Fatima, the Shah's daughter.

For a while Fatima and the Prince of Rubies lived happily together, but then Fatima became inquisitive about the life of the prince before they had met.

'I don't know anything about you,' she complained. 'Tell me who you are and where you come from.'

139

The Prince of Rubies went as pale as death.

'I cannot answer,' he whispered. 'Do not ask me such things, or you could lose me for ever.'

But the princess could not rest without knowing. One day when they were walking by a wide river, she asked the prince the same questions again. At once a mighty wave rose from the river and swept the prince away.

In vain Fatima ran along the river bank screaming for her lost husband. In vain the Shah had the river searched by the most skilled divers. It seemed that the Prince of Rubies had vanished into nothing.

Fatima fell into despair. She wept without ceasing and never stopped blaming herself for the loss of her husband. It was a very unhappy time.

Then one day one of her servants came to her with a strange story: 'Noble mistress,' said the girl, 'last night I couldn't sleep, so I went to stroll in the garden and sat for a while by the river.

'Suddenly I saw a troup of little genies who made a carpet of flowers on the lawn. They were followed by larger genies who spread a rug in front of the flowers and put a golden throne on the rug.

'Then the waters of the river parted and a grand procession led by an old man walked towards the throne. And the old man was leading by the hand a young man wearing a huge ruby on his forehead.

'The old man sat on the throne and the others danced on the carpet of flowers. The young man danced last of all, but he was pale and didn't seem to take any pleasure from the dance.'

The princess's broken heart was mended at once. 'That unhappy young man was my husband,' she said, 'I'm sure of it.' She decided at once to go with the servant the next night and watch in the very same place.

At midnight the waters of the river parted and a troup of genies appeared. They made the carpet of flowers and spread the rug and set up the golden throne.

Then, at last, the procession appeared. Fatima was shocked at how ill her husband looked, but she watched without speaking until the old man called for dancing to commence.

Then she ran forward and danced as she had never danced before on the lovely carpet of flowers.

'Marvellous'!' applauded the old man. 'I will grant you any request.'

'Then give me back my husband,' said the princess pointing at the pale young man.

'That is my son the Prince of Rubies and I am the King of the Rivers,' said the old man. 'Fatima, you have been punished enough for your bad behaviour. I will let your husband return to you.'

With those words he and his followers disappeared and only Fatima and the prince were left on the bank of the river, happy together and forever after.

141

# The Merchant and the Evil Genie

Many years ago in a great city in Persia, there lived a rich merchant. However this unfortunate man fell upon evil times. All his business failed. He lost his money and could do nothing but sit sunk in the deepest gloom.

Suddenly a genie appeared before him and said: 'My good merchant, would you like to have back all your riches?'

'Oh, if only it were possible,' sighed the merchant.

'It is. It is,' smiled the genie. 'Your troubles are over. All you have to do to be as rich as ever you were is to make me a simple promise. Promise that in eighteen years' time, you will bring back to this very spot and give to me the first living thing to greet you when you return home today.'

The merchant readily agreed. Eighteen years is a long time and, in any case, it was always his little dog which greeted him on his return home.

But of course, this time, it was not his dog, which greeted him, but his dear son, Ahmed. The merchant was heart broken, but what was done was done.

The genie kept his word. The merchant became rich again and in eighteen years' time he took his son to the spot where he had seen the genie.

However the merchant had told Ahmed the whole story and Ahmed was prepared. He had been to see a wise woman who had taught him how to draw a magic circle round himself so that nothing could harm him.

Ahmed surrounded himself with the circle before the genie appeared and so the genie could not take him away. Of course, the genie was furious.

'You have made a fool of me,' he shrieked to the merchant. 'But if I cannot have your son, neither shall you. It shall be his fate to go adventuring.' And so it was.

Ahmed left home and voyaged far across land and sea, until at last he came to a wild deserted shore where a mighty palace stood silent and alone.

But it wasn't quite empty. In the largest room on a massive throne of solid gold lay coiled an enormous serpent.

This terrifying monster spoke to Ahmed.

It said: 'I am the queen of this realm. A wicked spirit changed me into a serpent and so I must remain until a human being has the courage to spend the night in this palace without uttering a word. Have you the courage to do this for me?'

Ahmed agreed, and during the night twelve fearsome giants beat and tormented him, but he did not utter a single cry. The next day the serpent turned into a beautiful girl. Ahmed married the girl and became king.

For several years Ahmed lived happily in this kingdom by the sea, but then he became homesick and wished to see his parents again. He spoke to his wife the queen, who agreed that he should visit his home. She gave him a magic ring which would transport him wherever he wished to go.

'The ring will also bring to you anyone you wish to see,' she said, 'but never use it to send for me.'

Ahmed used the ring to travel home and then, forgetting his wife's warning, again used the ring to transport her to his parents' home, as they wished to see her so much. His wife was furious. She took back the ring and disappeared.

Ahmed set out at once to return to their palace. The journey took a very long time —that is, until he came into possession of a magic cloak, magic boots and a magic stick.

The cloak made the wearer invisible. The boots strode ten leagues at a time and the stick struck blows on its own. The owners of these useful things were quarrelling so much that Ahmed was able to take them without being seen.

He strode to the palace by the sea, put on the cloak and entered the palace unseen, set the stick to drive out the courtiers who were trying to turn his wife against him and then snatching off his cloak stood before the queen. How happy she was to see him again. They lived contentedly together as they had done before. Ahmed sent for his father and mother and restored the cloak and boots and stick to their owners. So all was well, for Ahmed never disobeyed his wife again.

# The Girl from the Pear Basket

Back in the olden days, people did not always pay their taxes with money. Sometimes they did what was called paying in kind. That is to say if they kept bees, they would supply the king with so much honey each year. If they kept sheep they would send the king so many fleeces each year and so on.

Once there was a man who had a fine pear tree. The king of that country was particularly fond of the type of pears grown on that tree. Instead of paying taxes, every year this peasant had to send the king four baskets of pears from the tree. The peasant was well pleased with this arrangement. It cost him very little work and he did not particularly like pears himself.

However, one year was a bad year for pears, as sometimes happens. There were not enough pears to fill four baskets. The peasant was afraid of the king's anger. He put his youngest daughter in one of the baskets and covered her with pears. That way it looked as if four baskets were full of fruit as usual.

The peasant took the baskets of fruit to the palace and the palace servants put them in the store room. They did not touch them for several days and in the meantime the little girl became hungry. She climbed out and nibbled at the food in the room.

The servants thought they had a mouse and searched round. To their surprise they found the little girl. By then it was too late to discover where she had come from, so the little girl was brought up in the kitchen with the palace servants.

They called her Viola because her eyes were as blue as violets.

The years went by and the little girl grew up into a beautiful young woman. She often played with one of the king's sons who was her own age and they became very fond of each other.

Viola might have grown up in the kitchen, but being in the palace, she could not help seeing the way the queen and the court ladies behaved. Viola wished to improve herself and made sure that her ways were as elegant and ladylike as those of the noble ladies.

Of course her pretty looks and her genteel ways and her friendship with the prince meant that Viola had enemies. People were jealous of her.

Two of the other serving maids started a rumour that Viola was a changeling and in league with the witches.

'We have heard her say that she visits the witches at night and that she knows how to get the witches' treasure,' they said.

This talk came to the king's ears. He was very interested. Witches were supposed to have great treasure and the king wished to have it for himself.

The king sent for Viola.

'I understand you know how to get the witches' treasure,' he smiled. 'Well, as I have given you a roof over your head and food to eat since you were a tiny child, wouldn't it be nice if you showed your gratitude by fetching the treasure and giving it to me?'

Poor Viola shook her head.

'I cannot, your majesty,' she gasped. 'I do not know anything about witches' treasure.'

This was true, but the king did not believe her. He thought she wanted to keep the treasure for herself.

The king had Viola thrown out through the palace gates.

'Do not show your face here again unless you bring the treasure with you,' he shouted, as the gates clanged shut.

Viola was very upset. The palace was the only home she had ever known and the prince was her greatest friend.

'There is only one help for all this,' thought Viola. 'I must find the witches' treasure, whatever it is and wherever it is.'

She set off on her quest.

First she passed an apple tree in bloom, but she did not stop there. Then she saw a peach tree in bloom, but she did not stop there. Then she saw a pear tree in bloom and, as night was falling, Viola climbed up into the branches and slept there for the night.

At dawn she was awakened by an old lady, who was the guardian of the tree. Viola told the kindly woman her sorry tale of woe.

'I will help you,' smiled the old lady. She gave Viola three loaves of bread, a bundle of millet, some dripping and some advice.

Viola thanked her and hurried on her way.

The path ahead led through a woodland and at last to a clearing where three women were trying to clean a stove. Viola gave them the bundle of millet and this cleaned the stove beautifully. The women were grateful and let Viola pass on her way.

Further along the path, three hungry dogs came snapping at Viola's heels, but she threw each of them a loaf of bread and this satisfied them.

The next obstacle in Viola's path was a broad, red river. Viola remembered the advice given her by the guardian of the pear tree.

'When you see a red river,' she had said, 'say it is beautiful and ask it to halt to let you pass.'

Viola did this and the river ceased flowing to let the girl walk across.

On the other side of the river was a huge castle, but the gates were stiff and would scarcely open. Viola rubbed the hinges with the dripping and at once the gates swung open before her.

In the grandest room of the castle, Viola found a small chest. She knew that inside was the witches' treasure. Picking up the chest, Viola turned to run back to the king's castle.

But the chest did not wish to be taken. It called to the gates: 'Slam shut! Slam shut!'

The gates replied: 'No. The girl was kind. She greased the hinges. We shall let her through.'

The chest did not give up. When they came to the red river it called: 'Flow fast. Flow fast. Do not let the girl cross.'

The river replied: 'She called me beautiful. I shall let her pass.' And it did.

The chest called to the fierce dogs to attack Viola, but they were full of food and asleep. It shouted to the three women to put Viola in their oven, but they would not.

At last Viola arrived safely back at the royal castle and was brought before the king. She handed the chest to him and when he opened it he found a chicken and her chicks, all of solid gold. Their value was immense and the king was delighted.

By this time the prince was standing at Viola's side. 'When my father asks what you would like as a reward, ask him if we may be married,' he said.

This Viola did. The king agreed and Viola and the prince lived happily ever after.

# Richard the Rascal

Once long ago, there was an urchin called Richard. He had no family and lived on the streets, keeping body and soul together as best he could. He was not always as honest as he should have been, but he had a twinkle in his eye and a charming manner and people like him.

The king of the little country came to hear of Richard and sent for him.

'Really you should go to prison because you have broken the law,' the king said. 'However I like you. If you can carry out some little tasks for me, I will pardon your crimes.'

'Very well, your majesty,' agreed Richard. 'What would you have me do?'

The king explained that a magician lived amongst the nearby hills. The magician owned a flying horse and the king would like the horse for his own.

'I will bring the horse for you within two days,' said Richard.

At once he went to the magician's house and crept into the stable by night. In those days animals were stabled on the ground floor and people slept in the rooms above. Richard started to bridle and saddle the horse, but it neighed loudly.

'Stop that noise, you stupid horse. Let me get my sleep,' called the magician.

'Surely you won't stay with a master who speaks to you so roughly,' Richard whispered to the horse. The horse went away with him at once. Richard took the flying horse to the king who was pleased, but immediately asked for something else, as is the way with kings.

'Now bring me the tablecloth belonging to the magician's wife,' instructed the king.

Richard went back to the magician's house where the wife was sitting working at the table, with the tablecloth spread on it.

'I have just seen your husband down in the valley being attacked by wolves,' said Richard.

It wasn't true, but it made the wife run out to help her husband and Richard was able to make off with the tablecloth which was very

valuable because it was made of cloth of gold.

'Very good,' smiled the king, 'but now bring me the magician himself. His magic powers could be very useful to me.'

Richard grew a beard and went to the magician's house and asked if he could enter and sit for a while by the fire. The magician agreed.

Richard looked round the room trying to think of a way to trap the magician. He saw a large box.

'What is the purpose of that box?' he asked.

'A rogue stole my horse and my wife's tablecloth,' said the magician. 'When I catch him I shall shut him in that box.'

Richard scoffed. 'The box isn't even big enough for an old man like you,' he said.

'Oh yes it is,' argued the magician and he curled up in the box to prove he was right.

At once Richard nailed down the lid and took the magician captive to the king. At this the king was satisfied and pardoned all Richard's crimes and made him rich for life. As for the magician, he soon used his magic to make his life at the castle comfortable, and his wife came to live with him. So all was well.

# The Legend of the Lilacs

The little Chinese girl, Mi, never had any toys. She had neither toys, nor cuddles, nor kisses, nor affection. Her mother and father had died when she was a baby and Mi had been taken in by distant relatives.

Poor Mi! From her earliest days, she had been made to work like a servant and in return she was given a bare mattress for a bed and a handful of rice for her meals. Her clothes were cast-offs. If she dared to sing, she was told to be quiet. If she stopped working for a moment, she was told to start again. She had to work hard for her keep.

Truly little Mi did not have a very happy life! However, one day, the Fairy of the Skies saw Mi kneeling in the garden crying. Her heart was touched and she wished to know what was wrong that the little girl should cry so much.

The fairy plucked a ray of sunshine and tossed it down to Mi.

'Hold tight to this thread of gold,' the fairy ordered.

Mi gripped the ray of sunshine and felt herself carried high up into the sky. Houses looked like doll's houses. Gardens were tiny green patches. Men and women looked like ants. Up in the clear blue sky, Mi's trouble seemed far away. She was happy for the first time in her life. The fairy spoke to her.

'I know your history,' she said. 'The breeze has told me how you cry in the garden, but now I will make you happy. I will give you wings so that you can fly through the sky like a bird. Your slavery is over. You are free.'

At a sign from the fairy, two genies of the heavens brought wings made of the most delicate gossamer.

Mi became a creature of the skies. She blew along with the clouds. She flew with the birds. She became a friend of the lovely white doves. On her pretty mauve wings she soared happy and free. And often she visited the Fairy of the Skies to thank her.

Alas! The North Wind became jealous of Mi. He stormed across the sky in a terrible rage and ripped Mi's fragile wings to pieces. The poor little creature fell tumbling to the earth and lay cold and still, with no life left in her.

The genies of the heavens came to weep over the body of the little girl and one tried to collect the pieces of her torn wings.

Behold! He found he was witnessing a miracle! Mi's torn wings had turned into the most beautiful flowers. They were that delicate mauve colour, which we call lilac.

That is why, ever since that far distant time, the lilac flowers have grown to be a memory of little Mi, who flew across the skies so happily, free at last from her life of hard work.

When the scent of the lilac blows across the land, the skies remember pretty little Mi.

# The Treasure of the Great Spirit

When young Prince Benar succeeded his father to the throne of an enormous kingdom in the far Eastern lands, he was just an irresponsible youth. With all the riches and power of being king in his hands, he spent his time in giving parties, putting on concerts and plays, going out hunting and picnicking and generally wasting away all his personal fortune and the money belonging to the state as well.

He wasn't a bad young fellow. He just didn't think. Good times were so much fun.

None of his ministers wanted to offend him by telling him he should pull himself together and spend some of his time working. Only his old teacher gave him a few sharp words:

'Take care, Benar,' he warned him, 'the wrath of the gods will descend on you if you do not mend your ways.'

But the young king turned a deaf ear to his old teacher and when he saw that the rest of the courtiers were laughing at him, the old man retired and went to live on the edge of a forest with his only daughter, Sarah.

Then one day when Benar happened to be alone in a room at the palace a dignified old man suddenly appeared before him.

'Benar! Benar! You are destroying yourself and you are destroying your people,' he said. 'I am the Great Spirit, king of the genies and king of the earth. So far I have protected your family, but now you have brought it to the brink of ruin.

'However, I will help you. Go into your father's old room. Lift a flagstone at the centre. You will see a mighty staircase. Go down it and you will find yourself in a room of treasure. But you must not touch any of the treasure until you do as will be told to you.'

The old man disappeared and at once Benar hurried to his father's room. He was short of money and longed to find the treasure. Down the long staircase he went.

Glittering treasure lay all around — and also a pedestal on which a statue should have rested, but there was no statue, only a note. It said:

'Before you touch the treasure, you must replace the statue by finding that precious thing which is the best in the world.'

Benar was puzzled. He did not really understand what he was supposed to do. The message was rather vague. He looked round hoping to see something which would help him.

A patch of air shimmered and waved like a white shadow in the dim light. Benar saw that it was his father standing peering towards him. Benar knelt down respectfully.

His father's voice came to him as if from a long distance in rising and falling waves of sound.

'Ask your old teacher for advice,' said the voice. 'Only he can help you.'

The vision shimmered and was gone. At once Benar leapt to his feet, went to the small house where the teacher was living and told him what had happened.

The old man listened carefully.

'That certainly isn't very clear,' he agreed. 'Fortunately I know the way to the home of

the Great Spirit. We must go there and ask him to explain exactly what you must do.'

The two men journeyed a very long way. They crossed hot deserts. They hacked their way through dark forests. They forded raging rivers and at last they came to a towering mountain at the top of which was a palace bleached white by the sun. Its doors were of glittering gold and its towers reached up into the swirling clouds.

The armed giants guarding the gates let the two men through. A shimmering genie took them to a walled garden — and there, sitting on a throne dazzling with diamonds, was the Great Spirit.

He listened to Benar's pleas and then this mighty spirit deigned to answer.

'Bring me a young woman without fault and I will tell you where to find the missing statue,' he ordered. He held out a cloudy mirror which reflected nothing.

'This mirror will only clear when a girl without fault looks into it,' he said. He turned away. Benar dared not trouble the Great Spirit further.

The two men had no idea where to start looking. They searched the world, but the mirror cleared for no one. At last thin, discouraged and exhausted they returned to the teacher's home.

'What a pretty mirror,' said his daughter, picking it up and smiling into its clear depths! She was the young woman without a fault.

The teacher was upset. He did not want to lose his daughter, but they took her to the Great Spirit. The Spirit smiled and he and the girl vanished. The lovely girl was lost to them.

Suddenly Benar was not interested in the treasure. He was in love with the girl, Sarah. Without her beside him the treasure was boring.

But the kingdom needed money and at last Benar went to the treasure room with his old teacher. On the pedestal was the missing statue covered with a veil and when Benar pulled it aside he saw Sarah, dressed as a queen and smiling at him.

The Great Spirit appeared and pointed at Sarah. 'Here is your wife,' he said to Benar. 'Before you could touch the treasure you had to learn that a pure heart is worth more than all the treasures of the world.'

And so Benar became a wise man, a great ruler and a happy one.

# The White Rabbit

Once there was a beautiful young noblewoman who lived in a very grand house surrounded by lovely gardens. The young lady was called Sylvia. She was very rich and had servants to work for her and wait upon her and noble friends who came to visit her.

There was really no need for Sylvia to stir from her fine house. Indeed she hardly ever went beyond her own gardens.

In this Sylvia was wise. Dark forests grew right up to the walls of the neat gardens. Fine folk only went out in groups or in their carriages with attendants to guard them. Humbler folk never walked out alone.

However, just once, on a day when the sun was shining and the forest did not look too grim, Sylvia walked through a gate in the garden wall and set foot amongst the trees.

She hadn't gone far when a white rabbit leapt into her arms. It was a sweet little thing with soft fur and lovely blue eyes. Sylvia fell in love with it at once. She cuddled it in her

arms and decided to take it home with her as a pet.

This was not a good decision because the white rabbit belonged to a woodland fairy.

Fairies are not known for their good temper and when the woodland fairy saw Sylvia walking away with her pet rabbit she was very cross.

Like a flash of fire the fairy swirled in front of Sylvia, blocking her path.

'You are a wicked girl to take my rabbit,' screeched the woodland fairy.

At once Sylvia tried to give the rabbit back. 'I'm sorry,' she said. 'I didn't know it belonged to anyone.'

'You don't suppose I want it back now you have been cuddling it,' screamed the fairy, who was enjoying being in a rage. 'You must keep it now *and* you must look after it properly. Remember it eats only four-leafed clover. If you feed it anything else it will die and then I shall come and take all your riches away from you.'

With that the fairy vanished and Sylvia hurried back to her house, carrying the white rabbit and wishing she had never seen it.

Four-leafed clover is not easy to find. Syl-via had to set all her servants searching for it from morning till night. For some weeks they managed to keep the white rabbit well-fed and healthy, but then there were no more four-leafed clovers anywhere the servants looked.

The white rabbit grew thin and sickly. In desperation Sylvia announced she would marry any young man who could find enough four-leafed clover to keep the white rabbit alive.

Of course all the single young men went out looking for four-leafed clover, but they had no luck. Just one young man called Martin *was* lucky. He found a little deer with an injured foot. Being kind, Martin stopped and helped the deer and the woodland fairy happened to be watching. She was in a good mood that day.

'You are a good young man,' she said to Martin.

'As a reward I will show you where the four-leafed clover grows.'

This she did. Martin took the clover to the white rabbit every day. Sylvia and Martin were married and they lived happily ever after.

# The King of the Lake

Long ago and far away in Japan, there lived a very brave warrior — brave but unlucky.

Whatever he touched went wrong. It was all very puzzling because Hido — that was his name — performed all his gallant deeds correctly, as he had been taught when he was a young warrior. However, he just did not seem to have that lucky touch.

If he slew a dragon, it was always the wrong one. If he rescued a maiden from a runaway horse, it always turned out she was a good horsewoman and meant to be riding that fast anyway.

If he were hired to drive bandits away from a village, they always turned out to be old friends of his and he would have to ask the villagers to hire another warrior, because he could not fight his friends.

In the end, word got around that hiring Hido was useless and everywhere he went, he met closed doors.

There was obviously only one thing to do. Hido must journey to a far country where no one knew him. He must start his warrior exploits all over again and this time he must be more careful.

Taking his long bow and his trusty sword Hido journeyed for many weeks until he reached a country he had never visited before. A wide lake lay in his path, but fortunately there was a bridge across it.

Not realizing this was a day which would change his life, Hido set off across the bridge. He had not gone far when he saw a huge serpent lying across his path.

Now, unlucky he might be, but Hido did not lack courage. Even though the body of the serpent was as thick as a mighty tree trunk and even though flames breathed from its nostrils, Hido stepped over it and went on his way.

He hadn't gone far, when he heard a voice calling to him.

'Hey, warrior!' it called.

'So they have talking serpents in these parts,' thought Hido, glancing back along the bridge.

However, instead of the hideous, slimy serpent, he saw a smiling man dressed in a blue robe and wearing a heavy crown of solid gold.

'Are you talking to me?' asked Hido, naturally feeling quite surprised.

'Indeed I am,' replied the man, 'you are just the person I have been looking for.'

The man in the golden crown went on to explain that he was the king of the lake. He ruled a crystal city down in the deepest depths of the water.

Until recently all had been happiness in his kingdom, but now he and his subjects were being terrorized by a ravenous dragon. Every night the dragon came to the lake's edge, dived down through the water and ate as many of the people of the city as it could catch.

'I have been looking for a brave warrior to fight this dragon,' explained the king. 'I saw you coming from afar off and I knew by your clothes and your long bow and your sword that you were a fighter. I turned into a fearsome serpent and lay in your path. When you stepped over me so bravely, I knew you were the warrior we needed to defend us.'

Hido was delighted.

'I am at your service, sire,' he said with a deep bow.

With that the king took Hido's hand and led him down to the depths of the lake. The waters parted in front of them. They came to a palace and city of pure crystal. They entered and were seated upon elegant furniture encrusted with pearls and rubies and were given delicious food to eat. Time slid happily by until all too soon *midnight came*!

There was a roaring like thunder. The waters of the lake boiled. The dragon had arrived. Hido snatched up his weapons and rushed up to the surface of the lake. Standing at the water's edge was a fearsome dragon, larger than anything Hido had ever seen before.

The warrior's courage did not fail. He drew his bow and shot an arrow. The aim was true, but the arrow glanced off the dragon's tough skin as if it were a dandelion seed blowing in the wind.

The dragon came closer to Hido, but he stood his ground and shot a second arrow. The dragon brushed it aside as if it were a buzzing fly.

By now the dragon was almost on him and in the excitement of the moment Hido remembered an old warrior telling him to lick the point of his arrow to make it fly true. He took his third and last arrow, licked the point and shot it straight between the dragon's eyes. The dragon gasped and fell dead. Hido's luck had changed.

The king of the lake was delighted and rewarded Hido with many riches. From that moment everything went right for the young warrior wherever he journeyed.

# Annette
# and the Seven Doves

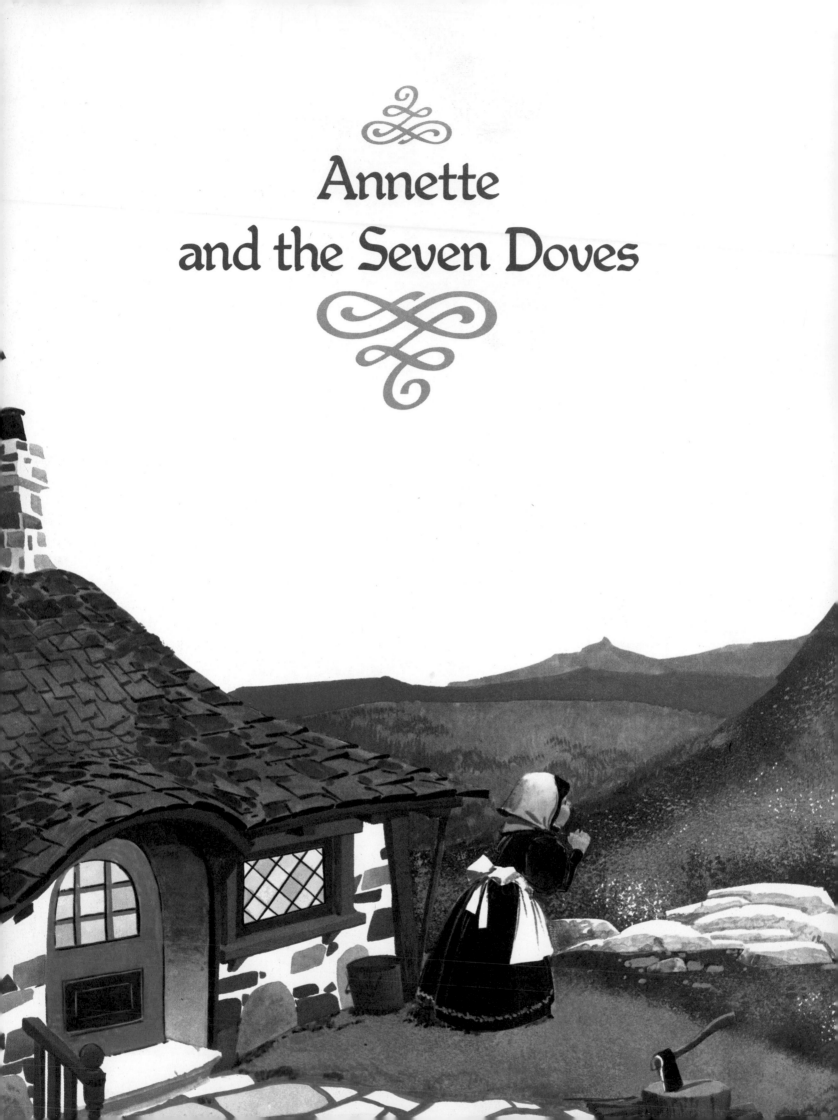

'Mother,' they said, 'we don't want another brother. You already have too much work to do. Why don't you ask for a little girl who could at least help you with the housework?'

The mother agreed, but she could not be sure that the woodland fairies would do as she asked.

'Well, if you are given another boy,' said the seven brothers, 'we shall leave home and try to earn our own keep in the great big world.'

The day came when the new baby was due to arrive. The seven brothers went out into the countryside as usual to fetch wood and collect berries.

'When it is time to come home, we will watch from the top of that hill,' they said. 'If the fairies bring a baby girl, put a distaff in the window, if it is a boy put an inkstand in the window. If we see the inkstand we will not come home, but go to seek our fortunes.'

Happily the fairies did bring a baby girl and the mother told a friend who was with her to put a distaff in the window. However the friend made a mistake and put the inkstand there instead.

The seven brothers were heartbroken, but they knew they could not be a burden on their mother any more.

Long ago in a far country, there was a good woman who loved children. She loved them so much that every year she asked the woodland fairies to bring her a new baby. She already had seven sons, and to feed and clothe them the woman had to work from dawn till dusk.

One year, as she was preparing to ask for yet another baby, her sons stopped her.

They walked for days, for weeks, for months, for years. At the end of three years they came to a forest where dwelt a blind ogre. It was because of a woman that the ogre had become blind and now he hated all women.

The seven brothers asked the ogre if he had need of help about the house and as he had it was agreed that they should work for him.

As time went by Annette — that was the name of the little sister of the seven brothers — grew up and her mother told her the whole sad story of her seven brothers who had left home because of a mistake. Annette decided to go in search of her brothers. It was a long and exhausting journey, but at last Annette came to the home of the blind ogre. She saw the seven young men working there, spoke to them and found that they were her long lost brothers. They all agreed to go home together.

However winter was almost upon them. 'We must wait till the spring to make that dangerous journey,' said the brothers to Annette. 'In the meantime you can stay here, but you must hide in one room. The ogre must never know that you are here. We will bring you food, but one thing you must always do is to give half your food to the cat we shall leave to keep you company.' Annette did as she was told, until one unfortunate day.

This day Annette found an almond in amongst her food. Without thinking she crunched it up and swallowed it without giving half to the cat. The large black cat was furious. It put out the fire which kept Annette warm. Annette ran out of the room to speak to her brothers. The ogre heard her voice and fell into a rage.

'What is a woman doing in this house?' he roared. He snatched up a knife and chased after the sound of poor Annette's voice. But the brothers led him out of the house and across the garden, where he fell into a ditch and broke his neck.

The brothers filled the ditch with earth and it seemed that they and Annette would be safe until the springtime, when they would be able to journey home and be with their mother.

'But there is one thing you must remember,' the brothers said to Annette. 'Pick nothing which grows on the earth over the ditch.'

Annette remembered these instructions until one day a poor beggar limped by.

'Please help me,' he asked. 'If you would pick some of those herbs growing in your garden and make them into a poultice for my leg, it would be better in an hour.'

Without thinking that the herbs were growing over the old ditch, Annette picked them, made the poultice and bound it to the beggar's leg.

The beggar was cured, but at once Annette saw seven white doves. They were her brothers transformed into birds because of her disobedience.

'What can I do?' she groaned.

'You must find the Mother of Time,' replied the doves. 'Only she can tell you how to help us.'

'I will find her even if I have to go to the ends of the earth,' promised Annette, and in spite of the bitter weather, she set out at once on her quest.

One day she came to the seaside and saw a big whale.

'Where are you going, my pretty?' he asked.

'Searching for the Mother of Time,' replied Annette. 'Do you know where she is?'

'Across that river and then ask the first person you see,' replied the whale. 'And when you do find the Mother of Time, ask her from me how I can avoid hurting myself against the rocks.'

On the other side of the river, Annette met a mouse, who told her the way, but then asked: 'And when you do find the Mother of

Time, ask her from me how I can rid myself of a pesky cat.'

Annette promised and went on her way until she met an army of ants. They told her to go down the mountain across the plain of flowers and then to ask her way of an old oak tree.

Annette did as the ants said and at last found herself speaking to an old oak tree.

'Walk on until you see a house on top of a mountain,' said the oak tree. 'That house is the home of Time,' continued the old oak tree, 'and when you speak to his mother, ask her from me how I can regain my honour which has been shattered by men who took my acorns and gave them to pigs to eat.'

On went Annette and, to her amazement, at the foot of the mountain she met the old beggar whose leg she had healed with the poultice of herbs.

'I will now repay you for the favour you did to me,' said the beggar. 'Up there you see the home of Time. Do not go up there until you have seen Time leave, or he will eat you. When he has gone, go up there and ask his mother the answer to all your questions.

'But first be very sure to take away the weights from the clocks on which she is sitting and secondly make her swear to tell you the truth by the wings of her son. No other promise will bind her.'

Annette scrambled up the steep mountain.

The house was a tumbledown old place. Summoning up all her courage, Annette went inside and snatched the weights from the clocks on which the Mother of Time was sitting. The clocks stopped. Time stood still and could not come to his mother's aid. Annette made the Mother of Time swear to tell the truth. Then she asked her questions and was given these answers:

'The oak will regain its honour when it gives up its treasure. The mouse need not fear the cat if it attaches a bell to its tail. The ants will live for a hundred years if they stop stealing things. The whale will find a safe route if it follows the sea rats. The doves will regain their human form when they alight on the tip of plenty.'

Annette ran back down to the plain. She called to the doves. 'Alight on the head of a bull, whose horns are the symbol of plenty.'

At once her brothers became human again. Annette spoke to the oak tree and it gave her the treasure buried amongst its roots. But the next night brigands stole the treasure and tied up Annette and her brothers. Then the ants came to their aid, chewing through their bonds and telling them where the brigands had hidden the treasure.

With the brigands chasing them, Annette and her brothers took the treasure and ran until they reached the sea — and there the whale came to help them.

Annette told him the answer to his question and in gratitude the whale told them to climb on his back. He took them along the coast out of reach of the bandits and soon they were safely home with their mother again.

How happy she was, and, with the help of the treasure from the oak tree, they lived in plenty for the rest of their lives.

# The Golden Bird

Many years ago, in China, it was the custom of men who wished to become monks to live in temples isolated from worldly things.

There was once such a temple in a lonely valley, surrounded by beautiful gardens. The monks lived their quiet lives, watching the seasons changing. They knew nothing but the wonders of the natural world and they were content to let the years roll by.

Then everything changed.

A young man was sent by his family to join the order of monks, but he himself did not want to live in a monastery. He kept talking about the comforts of the home he had left, the fashionable clothes brought by the travelling merchants, the interesting tales the merchants told of foreign lands.

All this talk made the temple and its garden seem very dull and uncomfortable.

Eventually the young man persuaded his family to let him return home. Several other monks did the same. Everyone was restless.

At last only five monks were left in the temple. Even they were discontented, but they had no families to which to return. They were afraid to leave the security of the only home they knew.

One day they were sitting in the garden, now overgrown and neglected, when a glittering golden bird flew above their heads. They had never seen anything like it before and they all stared as it twittered around them.

Suddenly five golden threads fell from the golden bird's claws. Each monk caught hold of a fluttering, twisting thread and then found he could not let go.

The monks had to follow wherever the magical bird led.

All through the world the monks were taken, their feet stepping with the swiftness of the wind and the lightness of air. They saw the pleasures of comfortable living, but also they saw the pain of war and strife. Finally the bird freed them back in the garden of their own temple. They looked around with relief. They would rather stay in the peace and safety of the temple and its gardens than roam out in the dangerous world.

172

# The Story of Six Brothers

Once there was a nobleman with six sons. They all lived together in a small castle in the country.

One day the father said: 'You boys should know better things than you can learn in a small country place like this. I will give you each one hundred silver coins and you must go out into the world and learn a useful skill. Come back here in a year's time and show me what you have learned.'

The brothers agreed. Going out to explore the big wide world is an exciting thing for a young man to do. As they rode out from home, they further agreed amongst themselves that they would meet together a month before they were due to go home to their father and they would tell each other what they had been doing.

Then each went his separate way.

The eldest brother fell in with an acrobat and spent his time learning how to make fantastic leaps and do clever balancing tricks.

The second son went to Switzerland and stayed with a carpenter who taught him how to make things from wood.

The third son learned how to play the violin so sweetly that anyone who heard him had to rise to their feet and dance.

The fourth brother learned the art of building fast and sea-worthy ships.

The fifth brother became an expert shot with a bow and arrow and, as for the sixth brother, he spent his time with a wise man and learned how to puzzle out difficult problems and how to foretell the future.

So eleven months went by and the brothers met each other as they had arranged. Each of them had learned a useful skill, but they were neither rich nor married, which to them seemed a pity.

'Well,' said the eldest, 'there is a month before we need go home to Father. Let us all try to become rich and find brides.'

They all agreed and the youngest said he had heard tell of a Princess Sophie who lived in a castle of pure gold, fastened to a rockside by four golden chains. A bell was attached to the chains and it would ring if anyone tried to free the princess. The castle was on an island and was guarded by a powerful dragon.

'Let us try to defeat the dragon and rescue the princess,' suggested the youngest son. 'She might be willing to marry one of us and in any case we should become rich from all the gold in the castle.'

This plan appealed to the adventurous young men. They hired a ship which had been made by the fourth brother and sailed at once to the island. On the advice of the sixth brother, who had been trained by the wise man, they quietened the bell by stuffing it with hemp.

The eldest brother, who had been trained by the acrobat leaped high to the top of the castle wall, balanced along a ledge and entered the castle. He found the princess and took her back to the ship.

Princess Sophie was very beautiful and was also glad to have escaped from the castle. The dragon had kept her prisoner since her father had died. The life there had been dull and dreary and she wished to get married and live on the mainland and have parties with young folk her own age.

Suddenly the sixth brother, who could foretell the future, looked serious.

'We must hoist sail and make our escape,' he said. 'Soon the dragon will discover the princess has escaped and he will give chase.'

The brothers would really like to have stayed and take treasure from the castle, but they felt so sorry for Princess Sophie that getting her away from the island seemed the most important thing to do.

They weighed anchor, but had hardly gone a few yards when the terrible dragon swooped over them. The fifth brother seized his bow and arrow and shot straight up into the dragon's body. He killed it with one shot and the dragon crashed to the deck.

Unfortunately the dragon was huge and heavy. Its scaly skin was hard and sharp. It cut through and shattered first the deck and then part of the hull of the ship. Water poured in and the vessel started to sink.

Princess Sophie screamed with terror. Had she been rescued from the dragon only to drown?

The second brother, who was a carpenter and the fourth brother, who was a ship builder, went frantically to work and repaired the ship just in time to prevent it from sinking.

However the shock had been too much for Sophie. She lay on the deck in a faint, pale and cold. It seemed that she would never open her eyes again. The third brother smiled and picked up his violin. He played the sweetest music ever heard.

Gradually a smile curved Sophie's lips. Her eyelids fluttered. She sat up. She rose to her feet and danced round the deck.

'I'm so happy to be free,' she laughed. 'I could dance for ever.'

With the dragon dead and Princess Sophie in her true health again, there was nothing stopping the brothers from going back to the island. They returned, loaded their ship with treasure and returned home rich men.

Needless to say, their father was pleased to see his sons returning with such wealth.

'But you only have one bride with you,' he said. 'Which of you is she going to marry?'

This was a puzzle. They had all helped to rescue Princess Sophie and she liked all of them equally.

Then the sixth brother, who could foretell the future, foresaw that he was the one most suited to make Princess Sophie happy. The other brothers, now being rich as well as young and handsome, soon found other young ladies willing to marry them.

There was a huge wedding party and the father felt he had done well to send his sons out to explore the great big world.

177

# The Frog Princess

Many years ago, the country we now call Russia was divided into many kingdoms and dukedoms. There were even huge areas with no particular ruler, but where wandering tribes grazed their herds.

In one of these far distant areas, near the edge of a mighty lake, there lived a chieftain with three sons. The chieftain's word was law. No one dared disobey him, least of all his sons.

One day the chieftain decided his sons were too big to live at home any more. It had been all very well when they had been little boys, but now they were big men.

The house always seemed to be full of them and their friends and too much noise. The chieftain wanted a little peace. He told his sons they must get married at once and go to live in homes of their own.

'But finding a wife takes time,' protested the eldest son, upset at the thought of having to run his own home, instead of lodging free with his father.

'Rubbish!' said the old chieftain. 'Each of

you shoot an arrow into the air and marry the girl nearest to where it lands.'

As the chieftain's word was law, so it had to be.

The eldest son shot an arrow and it landed at the feet of the daughter of a rich landowner, so everyone was quite pleased about that.

The second son shot an arrow and it landed near a young lady who owned many herds of cattle. That seemed satisfactory as well.

The third son shot his arrow and it landed in some swampy land near the edge of the lake. Not surprisingly, there were no young ladies standing about in that horrid, muddy patch of land, but there *was* a *frog*.

'Oh well,' said the third son, about to pick up the arrow, 'I suppose I had better try again.'

'No, indeed you will not,' said a voice.

The third son looked round in surprise and then realized with amazement that it was the frog talking.

'The arrow landed near me and you will marry me,' said the frog. 'I want to marry the son of a nobleman and you are a very handsome young man.'

The third son was confused. He didn't want to offend the frog, but marrying a frog seemed very unsuitable.

'Well, Miss Frog,' he mumbled, 'I'm sure you are very charming in your own way. However I'm equally sure my father expects me to marry a young lady and a rich young lady at that. It's been very nice chatting with you, but now I must go and shoot the arrow again.'

At that moment the chieftain and the other sons and their intended brides arrived to see where the third son's arrow had landed.

'No luck this time,' said the young man. 'I shall have to try again.'

The frog held on to the arrow and spoke up for herself. 'The arrow landed near me and he should marry me,' she said.

'Quite right!' agreed the chieftain, who wanted to get the whole affair settled.

'If you were foolish enough to shoot your arrow towards a swamp, then you must marry whatever lives in a swamp,' snapped the chieftain. 'The marriages will take place at once.'

As the first and second brother had found rich wives, the chieftain was not very bothered whether the third son married a wife with a fortune or not. He just wanted to get the marriages over and have his house to himself.

How everyone laughed at the third brother with his frog bride, but the marriages took place and each son went to live in a big house of his own and the chieftain enjoyed plenty of peace and quiet.

How pleasant it was having his meals on a tray in an easy chair, instead of having to provide a big banquet in the dining room every night. How enjoyable it was to be able to lock up and go to bed in a quiet house, instead of having to leave the doors open for his sons to come in late and often bring noisy friends with them.

But then the old chieftain fell to thinking. 'When I die I shall leave everything to my sons and their wives. I think they should make a fuss of me while I am still here.'

He went out for a ride and dropped in to visit his sons and hinted it would be very nice if his daughters-in-law each made him a hand-made shirt. They were so comfortable for an old man to wear.

The wives of the eldest two sons set to work, having a little laugh about what sort of shirt the frog bride would be able to make.

The third son felt quite glum. He looked at the frog.

'You will not be able to make a nice shirt for my father, so we shall fall out of favour with him and he will leave all his nicest possessions to my brothers and their wives,' he grumbled.

'Rubbish!' snapped the frog. 'Bring me some shirt material.'

The third son did as he was told. To his surprise, the frog tore the material into pieces and threw it from the window.

'Marvellous!' gasped the young man. 'Father will be pleased about that, I'm sure.'

Imagine his amazement when the wind came howling across the vast lake, snatched up the pieces of material, blew them round and round the house and then tossed them back in through the window, sewn into a simply beautiful shirt.

The chieftain was very pleased. He liked it much better than the shirts made by the other two brides.

'I think I will give a banquet,' he smiled. 'Peace and quiet is all very well, but I don't mind a party now and again and I should like to thank the young ladies for making me presents.'

A banquet was arranged and the brides of the two elder brothers giggled together about what the frog would wear.

'Perhaps some water weed sewn together,' they laughed.

However when the third son arrived, walking at his side was a beautiful radiant young lady in a lovely dress.

'I am so happy,' she smiled. 'I am the daughter of the king of the lake. My name is Princess Fenella. A water demon wanted to marry me. When I refused he turned me into a frog and said I should only regain my own form when I married a nobleman and was invited to a banquet. Now all that has happened and I am free from the spell,' she said, 'and to show how grateful I am I will use my magic powers.'

Shaking her sleeves Princess Fenella made visions of lakes and swans and trees and birds.

It was all great fun. The chieftain was very pleased and they all lived happily ever after.

# The Tree with the Leaves of Gold

Once upon a time there was a farmer so poor that all he could afford to give his three daughters was one little piglet each.

This certainly was not much. However, Little Clara, the youngest daughter, trying to make the best of her piglet, took it to feed on the lush grass which grew near a clear fountain.

There was a fine tree growing near the fountain and every day its leaves glittered in the yellow sunlight. One day Little Clara thought to take a close look at this brightly shining tree.

'Why, these leaves are real gold!' she gasped in amazement.

She picked two leaves. Surely two leaves would never be missed and two gold leaves would be such a help to her poor father!

But of course two leaves led to two more leaves and no doubt you can guess the rest. Soon the tree was bare of leaves altogether. Next it was the turn of the branches, which were made of gold also. Finally nothing was left of the tree but the trunk.

'Why leave that?' thought Little Clara. 'The trunk is no good on its own. I might as well have that too.'

She took an axe and with a well-aimed blow, cut the tree trunk to the ground.

To her amazement, where the tree had stood there appeared a marble staircase. Little Clara did not hesitate. She ran down the stairs and found herself on a huge plain in front of a magnificent castle. In she went and found a grand room with a table covered with dishes of delicious food.

As she was hungry Little Clara picked up a cake, but she had only taken one bite, when a black monster appeared before her.

'Don't be afraid,' said the monster. 'No one will hurt you, so long as you do not try to leave here nor ever light a candle during the night.'

So Little Clara was a captive, but she was in a golden prison. The monster, who was called Benjamin, gave her clothes fit for a princess, magnificent jewellery, a carriage to ride in and a whole horde of servants.

Alas! Curiosity overcame Little Clara. One

night she lit a candle and in the place of the monster, she saw a handsome young man lying asleep. Woken up by the light he leapt to his feet.

'You stupid girl!' he shouted. 'All because of you I shall have to stay another seven years in the shape of this monster. Get out of my sight!'

Little Clara fled, miserable and sorry. Luckily a good fairy saw her distress.

'Here are seven spindles and seven pairs of shoes all made of iron,' said the fairy. 'You must walk on and on until you have worn out all the seven pairs of shoes. Then you will see seven women sitting on a balcony and spinning with spindles of bone.

'You must replace the bone spindles with these iron ones, but you must not let the women know what you have done until they have sworn not to harm you. They are Benjamin's sisters and their mother is a witch.'

Little Clara set out walking and all befell as the fairy had told her. She found the women on the balcony. She put the iron spindles in place of the bone ones. She made the women promise not to harm her. But of course the *witch* had not promised not to harm her.

She said to Little Clara: 'Here are twelve sacks full of peas and lentils and haricot beans. If you haven't picked them over by this evening, I will make you disappear into thin air!'

Terrified, Little Clara set to work, but she soon saw the task was impossible. Then, as seven years had passed, Benjamin came home, freed from his enchantment. He called up an army of ants who sorted the sacks of beans in one hour!

But then the witch, Benjamin's mother, set Little Clara the task of filling twelve mattress covers with feathers before nightfall the next day or she would make her vanish forever. Little Clara turned again to Benjamin.

Benjamin felt that Little Clara had suffered quite enough and once more he came to her aid.

'Spread out the mattress covers on the ground,' he said. 'Then tear your hair and rend your clothes and sob and weep that the king of the birds is dead.'

Little Clara did as Benjamin said and when the birds of the air heard her, they came in their thousands. There were so many that they darkened the sky and in their grief they plucked the feathers from their breasts and the feathers fell to the ground more than enough to fill the twelve mattress covers.

The witch was furious, but she hid her feelings.

'Very good!' she smiled wickedly. 'Now go and find my sister. Ask her to give you the musical instruments, as I wish to give a party, as my son says he wants to marry you.'

Benjamin stopped Little Clara along the road.

'All this is a trick,' he said. 'My mother's sister is an ogress. She will greet you with a baby in her arms and ask you to hold it while she fetches the musical instruments. While she is gone you must put the baby in the cellar, take the musical instruments from behind the door and escape as swiftly as you can.'

Little Clara bravely did as she was told and returned safely.

The witch could think of no more tricks to trap Little Clara and roared with rage, but she had to let the wedding take place.

Little Clara married handsome Benjamin and they lived happily ever after — especially as Little Clara gave up being so inquisitive.

However, happy as she was with Benjamin, Clara did feel that he had some very undesirable relatives.

'I think that as your mother does not appear to like me and as she is a witch, I ought to learn a little magic — just in self defence, you know,' she said to Benjamin.

Benjamin did not seem to consider the matter at all serious.

'Now that we are married, Mother will love you like a daughter,' he smiled.

'Perhaps so,' replied Clara, but she did think to herself that she would prefer to be on the safe side.

'And what about your aunt who is an ogress?' asked Clara. 'Have I nothing to fear from her?'

'Perhaps Auntie can be a little difficult at times,' agreed Benjamin.

He took Clara to visit a Good Fairy and said she should be taught a spell against ogresses.

'And also a spell against witches,' whispered Clara, while Benjamin was looking out of the window.

So Clara learned spells to keep herself safe and had no more trouble from anyone.

# The Winged Horse

In the days when miles of dark forest smothered the countryside, strange monsters such as the Chimera lurked in the faraway thickets.

Wise men stayed in the sunny, open glades and left the deep forest to keep its own secrets.

However all men are not wise and one unlucky year a great lord cleared vast tracts of the forest in order to have more room to graze his animals.

Disturbed by the work of the foresters, the Chimera came forth to terrorize the countryside. It had a lion's head with which to maul people. It had a horse's body with which to run fleetly after them. It had a long serpent's tail with which to seize and crush people. It breathed fire and spread fear.

It was also that for which Lord Bellerophon was searching.

This unfortunate young man had slain his brother in a hunting accident. He was overcome with grief and felt he could only make amends by passing through terrible danger himself to do good to others.

'I will rid the world of this terrible creature or perish in the attempt,' he smiled.

However his father did not wish to see Bellerophon killed. He gave him instead a magical horse with wings of white feathers to ride. Down almost into the very jaws of the Chimera swooped Bellerophon and flung a lance straight and true.

The Chimera perished. The people rejoiced and Bellerophon smiled once more.

# The Magic Gifts

Russia is a very big place. On its eastern side there are miles and miles and miles of woodlands where very few people live.

Amongst all those millions of trees, there are a few large lakes and at the side of these lakes little family groups of people manage to make a living.

One such family was called Rostov and Dimitri was the son of the family.

It was Dimitri's job to push the family boat out on to the lake and catch fish for the family dinner.

Now making roads in those parts was very difficult. It meant cutting down so many trees.

If folk wanted to go from one lakeside village to another, they often rowed across by boat.

One day, just as Dimitri was setting out fishing, a girl asked him if he would row her to a house on the other side of the lake.

'I am Olga,' she said. 'I am new here. My parents have died and I have come to live with my aunt in the log house a mile along the lakeside.'

The girl was very beautiful and much better dressed and more sparkling than any of the country girls Dimitri had met before. By the time he had rowed her across the lake he was in love with her. He asked her to marry

him, thinking that if he wasted any time, such a smart girl would be snapped up by someone else.

Now Dimitri was a handsome boy and the girl agreed to marry him, but on one condition.

'I am used to town life,' she said. 'It all seems pretty dull and boring here in the country. You must find for me as a present, something really magical and out of this world. Something to make my life easier than having to work from morn till night.'

'Oh yes, yes, of course I will,' agreed Dimitri, so eager was he to have such a fine girl as his wife.

So the next day, Dimitri journeyed to the lake's end and then further and further along the only rough road and then up a track through the trees until he came to the home of a wise woman.

'I must have something with magical powers to give to my bride,' he said.

'I have the very thing,' smiled the wise woman.

She gave Dimitri a young lamb and told him that whatever he wanted, all he need do was ask the lamb for it and it would appear.

Dimitri was naturally very pleased and set

off home with the lamb. However night fell and he had to take a room at an inn. When he was in his room, Dimitri looked at the lamb and said:

'Little lamb, little lamb, put on the table a nice steak and kidney pie, a bowl of strawberries and cream with plenty of sugar and a bottle of wine.'

At once all these nice things appeared on the table. Dimitri was delighted with everything. He ate his fill and went to sleep. Unfortunately the innkeeper had been spying through the door and had seen what had happened.

During the night he stole the lamb, put an ordinary one in its place and said nothing.

Dimitri knew he had the wrong lamb as soon as he woke, but he could prove nothing, so he went back to see the wise woman again.

She must have been patient as well as wise, because she gave him another gift. This time it was a handkerchief.

'Whatever you desire, wave this handkerchief and say what you want and it will appear,' she said.

Once more Dimitri set off for home. Once more darkness fell and once more Dimitri took a room at the inn. He shut himself in his

room and waved the handkerchief over the table.

'I want bread and a bottle of wine and fish and chips and jam sponge pudding with custard,' he said.

At once this delicious meal appeared on the table. Unfortunately again the innkeeper was watching and again while Dimitri slept the innkeeper crept in and stole the handkerchief. Again Dimitri could prove nothing.

Dimitri went back to the wise woman and told her what had happened. Again she gave him a gift or rather two gifts. She gave him two strong sticks.

'Go back to the inn for the night,' she said. 'Hide one stick in your bed. Put the other stick on the table. Ask the stick on the table to bring you food and it will, but when the innkeeper comes to steal that stick, the second stick hidden in the bed will beat him till he does as you ask.'

Very well pleased, Dimitri went back to the inn and did as the wise woman had told him. In the middle of the night the innkeeper crept into the room, tried to steal the stick from the table and was beaten by the stick from the bed.

'Stop that stick!' he shrieked. 'Stop that stick. I will do anything, but stop that stick!'

'Give me back my lamb and give me back my handkerchief,' said Dimitri, 'and then I will stop the stick from beating you.'

The landlord gave the lamb and handkerchief back at once and in the morning Dimitri went on his way taking the four gifts from the wise woman.

He went to the log house where Olga lived and gave her the magical presents. Olga was very pleased. Now she could lead a comfortable life, instead of her usual hard life.

Olga and Dimitri were married very soon and lived happily for a hundred years. They stayed in the forest because this was the life Dimitri was used to. And Olga was happy because everything she wanted was brought to her by the lamb or the handkerchief or one of the sticks.

# King Midas

Many hundreds of years ago, near that part of the world we now call Greece, there lived King Midas. In those days there were many gods and goddesses. Their home was on Mount Olympus. They were beautiful and powerful and proud and full of magical tricks. Most humans were frightened of them, but King Midas was a big jolly fellow and saw no reason why the gods should do him any harm.

King Midas liked mixing with the gods and inviting them to dinner, which was all very understandable. The gods were so clever and witty and amusing and dazzling in their beauty that being with them was a wonderful experience.

King Midas forgot how dangerous these beautiful creatures could be.

One evening King Midas entertained Bacchus the god of wine and Pan the god of woods and shepherds to a very jolly dinner. Afterwards Bacchus said he would grant King Midas any wish he liked.

Now, being a king and entertaining important people is very expensive. For his wish, King Midas asked that everything he touched should turn to gold.

'This way I shall never be short of money,' he thought.

Bacchus granted the wish. At first King Midas was pleased. He touched the flowers in the garden and they turned to gold. He touched a bush and a tree and a wall. They all turned to beautiful, glittering gold. However when King Midas became hungry and wanted to eat, his *food* turned to gold. He could not eat. His daughter ran to put her arms round him and she turned to gold.

King Midas was broken-hearted. He was learning how dangerous it was to mix with the gods. However Bacchus took pity on him and reversed the wish. The golden objects became as they had been before and King Midas was happy. Not for long, however — King Midas could not resist the exciting company of the gods. He agreed to judge a musical contest and unfortunately offended Apollo, the sun god, by not giving him first prize.

Apollo said nothing and swept out of the room, but he had left a curse on unfortunate King Midas.

The servant who took care of the king's hair first noticed the trouble.

King Midas was growing ass's ears.

At first the servant combed the king's hair to hide the pointed ears which were starting to prick up. At last nothing could hide them. King Midas was distraught. He shut himself up in his room and made the servant promise to tell no one of his shame.

For a while the servant obeyed, but keeping a secret is a terrible burden. When he could bear it no longer, the servant dug a hole in the ground and whispered into it: 'King Midas has ass's ears.'

Then the servant went away happy, thinking he had done no harm, because he had told no *person* about the king's dreadful affliction.

However grass grew from the earth over the hole and Apollo caused the wind to blow through the grass and the grass whispered: 'King Midas has ass's ears. King Midas has ass's ears.'

Soon the whole kingdom knew the king's secret and was laughing at him. King Midas was a figure of fun until he managed to persuade Apollo to forgive him and make his ears human again.

Mixing with the gods can be dangerous.